WOUNDED BUT VICTORIOUS

After three agonizing years of surgeries and rehab, U.S. Army veteran Jason Donahue is ready to leave the Iraq War in the past and rejoin society. Yet, no matter the success he achieves at work, people wince every time they see him.

Everyone but Emily Riley. From the first, the beautiful redhead looks past his disfigurement and sees *him*. In return, Jason wants to buy her everything she deserves, starting with her dream home and going from there. Yet Emily has scars of her own, a past she's not ready to reveal. Only when they both come clean, when they view each other through eyes of trust and love, will they know that, when a good man and a good woman give each other their heart, the two will always have more than enough.

UNEXPECTED ASSETS

A Texas Hill Country Romance

Emily Mims

www.BOROUGHSPUBLISHINGGROUP.com

UNEXPECTED ASSETS
Copyright © 2015 Emily Wright Mims

ISBN 978-1942886-49-5

Except for the military academies themselves, the Corps of Cadets at Texas A&M University trains and commissions more military officers than any other university in the nation. Aggies have served in every branch of the military, and many have paid a high price protecting our freedom. I would like to dedicate this book to every Aggie who has ever served our nation, with special thanks to those who have paid the ultimate price for America.

Table of Contents

UNEXPECTED ASSETS

Chapter One

Emily Riley hummed along to her favorite rock station as she dug around in her drawer looking for the lace teddy she bought last month. Damn, where was that thing? She flipped through her entire lingerie drawer twice without success then opened the drawer that housed her shorts and sweaters. Nope, not there either. It had to be somewhere.

Biting back a curse, she pulled open the bottom drawer she had cleared out for Jason a couple of months ago and pawed through his boxer briefs and T-shirts, finally spotting the elusive teddy lurking between two pairs of his silky boxers. "Gotcha," she said triumphantly as she pulled out the naughty confection of black satin and lace and smoothed down his pile of underwear.

Smiling, she folded the teddy that made Jason's mouth water. Then, remembering what he whispered when he thought she'd fallen asleep, her heart clenched. *So fine and expensive; too beautiful for the likes of me.*

Burying the pain along with the teddy, she closed the small suitcase she'd packed to go to her parents' home in San Antonio for Thanksgiving. She didn't really expect to have a chance to wear it. She'd never brought home a boyfriend before so she didn't know for sure, but she would bet her spring tuition that her mother, Patsy, wouldn't allow Jason in the same wing, much less in the same bedroom with Emily, especially since they were not formally engaged.

Then there was her sister Holly, her beau Jimmy and his daughter Carrie. Holly had flat-out moved in with Jimmy to care for him while he recuperated from a grenade explosion, set off by the madman known as Chucky, that had almost cost Jimmy and Holly their lives. Surely, Patsy wouldn't try to put the lovers in separate bedrooms now.

Emily's mouth curved as she thought of the beaming smile on Holly's face when she had shown off the goat-choking diamond Jimmy had put on her finger. "I love it," Emily had told her sister as she admired the ring.

"I love *him*," Holly had replied. "The ring's just icing."

Emily riffled through the closet looking for her blue church dress before she remembered that it was still in San Antonio, along with most of the rest of the dressier clothing she didn't need as a student at Texas A&M. But those days would be coming to an end, she noted, looking down at the shiny gold senior ring on her right hand. Just a little while longer and she would either be in graduate school or employed somewhere working in a medical research laboratory.

She made a face as she checked her traveling diabetes kit. It was the underlying reason for her interest in medical research; she hoped that someday she could work on improving the lives of diabetics like her.

She might as well check her blood sugar while she was thinking about it or Jason was going to fuss at her when he got home. Lancing her finger, she put the sample on the test strip. Two-hundred twenty-five. Damn. Her blood sugar, a pain in the ass to begin with, had never settled down since the same madman who nearly killed Jimmy and Holly had injected Emily with a massive dose of insulin in an attempt to murder her and Jason almost a month ago.

She had passed out quickly and had no real memory of the experience, but Jason, who already suffered from the occasional nightmare from his time in the war, now had the attack to add to his list of nightmares. Plus, his ribs were still sore and the already delicate skin of his massive burn scars was just now healing.

Even still, she and Jason had a lot to celebrate, she thought with satisfaction. They were going to be all right, Holly and Jimmy were going to be all right, and tonight she was celebrating the acquisition of her senior ring. And after that? Was Jason going to—?

Emily's musings were interrupted by the cheerful notes of the Beach Boys' 'Surfin' USA', her mother's ringtone. "Hi, Mom," Emily said brightly as she pictured her sweet-faced mother on the other end of the phone. "Whatcha know that's good?"

Patsy Riley laughed. Emily always greeted her mother with the familiar question. "Well, let's see. All three of my children are going to be home for Thanksgiving, Holly's bringing her new fiancé and her new daughter, you're bringing your sweetie, and Russ has promised not to start any arguments with his father or grandfather."

Although Holly was Ben Riley's daughter by his first wife, Patsy had reared Holly along with Russ and Emily and loved Holly as if she were her own. Holly was prepared to do the same for Jimmy's motherless daughter Carrie.

Emily laughed out loud. "You really believe that? Russ in the same room with Daddy and Granddaddy and no arguments? Mom, what planet did you say you just teleported in from?"

Patsy joined Emily in laughing. "I said Russ promised not to *start* any arguments. He didn't say he wouldn't finish one. Frankly, I'm not worried about any of them; they can all three hold their own. So what about Jason? Is he ready to face the entire Riley clan?"

"I think so," Emily said. "He faces just as much chaos on the sales floor every day and it doesn't seem to faze him."

"So they did move him," Patsy said. "That night we took you out to dinner he said they had threatened to."

"Yes, they moved him a week or so later and he's doing just as well as when he was doing Internet sales. I guess the Blakely customers are more accepting of the scarring than Mr. Blakely thought they would be. Jason owes Holly a big one for getting him that job." Holly, a wounded warrior like Jason, went to Fred Blakely and pled Jason's case when Blakely was reluctant to hire a badly disfigured salesman to work the sales floor at his car dealership.

"But Jason's paying it forward," Patsy reminded Emily. "His support group is almost as big as Holly's, isn't it?" Holly had also helped Jason with organizing a wounded warrior's support group there in College Station similar to the one she headed at Heaven's Point.

"It's actually bigger. And Jason's a really good resource for his group, since most of them are A&M students trying to go back and get their degrees like he did. Seeing how well Jason's doing these days and the money he's making gives them hope that they can do the same."

"Speaking of money, have you said anything to him yet?"

Patsy's voice was deceptively casual but Emily was not fooled. "Nope. Not a thing. And I'm not going to, not until I have a declaration of undying love and a ring on my finger." Emily winced at the tartness in her tone. "Sorry if I sounded cold, Mom. Didn't mean to."

Patsy sighed. "I hope to hell you know what you're doing, hon. It's going to be a shock to him when he finds out."

"I'm doing what I have to, Mom. If he loves me, Jason will understand." He would understand, Emily promised herself. He had to, if their relationship had any chance of succeeding.

"I hope so." The pause said it all, Patsy wasn't so sure. "So what time do I look for you on Thursday?"

"Actually, I don't have class tomorrow and Jason took an extra day off. We should be there tomorrow early in the afternoon."

"Wednesday instead of Thursday. That's wonderful," Patsy enthused. "Well. If both you and Holly are getting here tomorrow I better go make up some beds. See you tomorrow."

"Bye, Mom." Emily looked at the time on her phone. She needed to get ready for the evening.

She took a quick shower and donned her favorite skinny jeans and a tight biscuit-colored sweater that clung to her chest. Her round face, riot of freckles, and carrot-red hair might not be considered pretty, but even she was willing to admit her figure was nice; long legs, a shapely backside, a flat stomach and pinched-in waist to go with her rather decent breasts, if she must say so herself. Perhaps it was the exercise she loved, perhaps it was the strict diabetic diet; her muscles were long, toned and in all the right places. A lot of women would have willingly taken on her looks to get the figure and would have been glad. But those women had never made the mistake of loving someone like Brandon Bentley and had their egos shredded royally.

Where did that come from?

Deep-sixing any thoughts of that shithead, Emily found the pretty pearl choker Jason had surprised her with and added it to her ensemble. She put on her usual mascara and blush and was glossing her lips when she heard Jason boom, "Where's my woman?"

"Right here," she said as she sashayed into the living and wound her arms around his neck. "Just like I am every day."

Jason picked her up and whirled her around the room. "Jason, your ribs," she protested as he scooped her up in his arms.

"I'm fine, Emily. They hardly hurt anymore."

"Well, in that case," she wound her legs around his waist and let him hold her. "So give me a kiss and tell me how your day was."

Jason lowered his head and met her lips. As always, she reveled in the feel of his powerful arms around her as they clung together for long moments, their kiss exchanging the promise of more sweetness to come. Finally he raised his head and smiled at her. "So is tonight going to have to hold us until Sunday, or have your parents joined the twenty-first century?"

"I talked to Mom today but didn't have the nerve to ask her," she admitted. "I think they know you spend more time here than you do at your own place next door, but that's here, not under their roof. And it's going to be interesting seeing what sleeping arrangements they've made for Holly and Jimmy, since Holly's moved in with him."

"Has Holly given you any more updates, by the way?" he asked as he put her down and picked up a cardboard cylinder leaning on the wall by the door. "Other than the headache's gone and Jimmy's stitches out?"

"Holly still can't remember anything about what happened in the attack or for most of the rest of the day, and they don't expect her to. Jimmy's still recovering, but the doctors said he should be fine. Holly says the only recurring problem seems to be the nightmares from hell to go with the rest of his PTSD."

"Did he scar up real badly?" he asked as he sat down at the table and pulled a large square of thick paper out of the cylinder. Jason knew scars. While he had been able to keep all of his fingers, the scars made his hands stiffer than normal, but he had almost complete use of them.

Emily made an exasperated sound. "Do you really think either of them gives a damn about that?" She leaned over and kissed Jason's badly scarred cheek. "They're alive and going to be all right and that's all that matters." Switching gears—she hated to dwell on the scar issue—she looked at the paper and shrieked. "Oh, wow, are those the plans for your new house?"

Reaching out, he patted the chair next to his. "Do we have a few minutes before I have to get ready to go? I want to show them to you."

"We have plenty of time," she said as she sat down. He unrolled the neatly drawn plans. "Turn them around so that the front door is facing me."

Jason gave the plans a quarter turn. "These are just preliminary. The architect can change anything we want changed before he draws up the actual blueprints."

'We' want changed? Jason, what are you saying to me? She reached out and traced the path up the sidewalk to the front door. "Nice big front porch," she said admiringly. "What direction is the house going to face?"

"If I get that lot we looked at last Sunday, the front door will face almost due north and the big back patio will get the full effect of sunset. Hot in the summer but there are enough oak trees to provide shade from about two in the afternoon on." He pointed to the middle of the plans. "Tell me what you think of the inside."

Emily took a few minutes to study the architect's layout. "The entrance and living room are well laid out and have good traffic flow." She traced her finger over the plans, envisioning where guests would enter and leave the rooms. "Movement into the dining area works, too." Her finger kept moving as she 'walked' into a large great room, where the architect had sketched a massive fireplace on the inside wall and a galley kitchen and breakfast area on the opposite side of the room.

"Hmm, something you might want to think about. Your architect's put the fireplace on the inside wall, which isn't a bad place for it, but the kitchen is backed up to an outside wall and just has one tiny window, which is going to make the room dark and gloomy. If the plumbing isn't a problem, you might want to have him reverse the room, put the fireplace on the outside wall, and put big windows or doors on either side of the fireplace. The room will be much brighter, plus, the kitchen will back up to the garage for unloading groceries. And, you have the potential of making the fireplace two-way, with a second hearth on the wrap-around part of the patio."

"Great ideas. He whipped out a notepad and wrote *Flip great room and do outside fireplace* in big letters. "Keep going."

Emily looked over the rest of the house plan. As she shared her thoughts with him, he added them to the notepad in front of him until she objected. "Jason, this is going to be your house. You should be more worried about what you think than what I think."

"No, I shouldn't," he said easily. "I really do want to know what you like and don't like about it."

Was he thinking in terms of the two of them living there together? He hadn't come out and said so, but he had taken her with him to look at lots and involved her in every step of the planning process so far. He couldn't intend to live in that big, four-bedroom house by himself, could he?

"So did we use up all our time on the plans or do I have time to do a little packing before I shower?" he asked as he rolled up the drawing and put it back in the cardboard cylinder.

"A few minutes, sure," she said.

Jason laid his beat-up old suitcase down on the bed and quickly had his underwear and a long-sleeved robe packed. He packed a couple of pairs of khaki pants then counted out enough pairs of jeans to last the weekend.

Emily looked at his choice of T-shirts and frowned. "Jason, you don't have anything here but long sleeves. It's going to be over eighty degrees this weekend. You know you have to stay cool or you're going to overheat and make yourself sick."

"It's supposed to get cooler," he said tightly. "I'll be just fine in the long-sleeved shirts."

"No, you won't," she said firmly, reminding him of what he surely knew. "You're missing sweat glands in over fifty percent of your body. You can't regulate your body temperature worth crap. If you get overheated and pass out you're too damn big for me or anybody else in the Riley family to pick up." At six-four and well over two hundred pounds, Jason towered over the Riley men and was considerably heavier than Holly's lanky love Jimmy Adamcik. "And if you believe the weather report, I'll sell you that Arizona swamp you've had your eye on." She softened her face and her expression. "Jason, they don't care about the scars."

Jason looked down at the pile of shirts, took a deep breath then muttered, "I guess you're right. My arms aren't any worse than what's left of my face. But I have to take a few long sleeves and a hat or two to keep the sun off the damn…"

"Of course," she flinched at the bitterness in his tone. But he was being realistic. There was nothing left of his face but scar tissue; his ears and hair were also casualties of the catastrophic burns he had suffered in Iraq trying to save a little boy strapped with explosives. Even though he'd had a number of years to adjust to his new appearance, he'd been so self-conscious when they first met that for months he'd ignored her obvious interest in him, until Holly gave him a much-needed shove in Emily's direction.

Time had healed some of his emotional wounds. Now, at ease enough to work a showroom floor as a car salesman—a good one, if his checks were anything to go by—and to strip down in front of her without flinching, as he had the first few times they had been naked together, overall he had made amazing progress in the five months they had been a couple. But, sometimes, insecurities reared their ugly head and Emily could tell he still mourned the loss of being a handsome man.

Well, who wouldn't?

They'd work on it, she vowed, starting with short-sleeved T-shirts. Jason found several of the shirts she insisted he wear then helped him match them up with the long sleeved button-downs he would wear over them in out in the sun. They made quick work of the rest of his packing and he shed his work clothes into the hamper.

"I'll hurry in the shower. Go check with those yahoos next door and see what time they want to leave."

"They're not yahoos and you don't need to hurry," she said as she walked past him and patted his delicious well-muscled backside, giving it a sexy little swat as he reached around and snagged her for a long, sweet kiss before he disappeared into the shower.

In spite of the burns and the scarring, Jason had a fantastic, hard-muscled body that he kept fit with regular workouts. In tight jeans and a long-sleeved shirt his body looked better than most.

His incredible body attracted Emily; his bright blue eyes, quick wit, and gentle smile won her heart. Of course she noticed the scars; they were pretty hard to miss. But they became minor because she *saw* Jason.

Chapter Two

Emily pulled on a pair of tooled cowgirl boots and ran a brush through her hair. She slipped a matching cardigan over the sweater and in a minute was banging on her neighbors Wade and Benny's front door. "Hey, guys, Jason wants to know when you want to leave."

Wade Baxter was in the process of pulling on a T-shirt as he yanked open the front door. Tall, good-looking Wade and his even taller, teddy bear-like roommate Benny had been her next-door neighbors since their freshman year as Aggies. And they had proved to be wonderful friends to her.

Ironically, they were both from the same little Hill Country town that her sister Holly and brother Russ now called home. Holly had become very good friends with Wade's mother Angie, and Benny's brother Rory worked in the same sheriff's department as her brother Russ.

Wade straightened his T-shirt and checked the time on his cell phone. "Fifteen minutes at least. Benny's still in the shower."

"So's Jason." Emily spotted the two big baskets of dirty laundry sitting with their suitcases in the middle of the living room floor and rolled her eyes. "Wade, really? Haven't you and Benny grown up enough to do your own laundry?"

Wade grinned unrepentantly. "You honestly think my mom does my laundry?"

Benny, clad in what looked like his last pair of jeans, stepped out of the bathroom and started pawing through a pile of clothes on the sofa looking for a T-shirt and socks. "We ought to get us a sweetie to do ours. Emily here does Jason's up really nice and Lisa won't let Rory touch his. Ya think Lisa will keep doing it for him after the wedding?"

Emily groaned and moved on to another topic. "I heard Jimmy and Holly working on the wedding music together. They sound pretty good."

Wade glanced over at the wall separating the two halves of the duplex. "Speaking of, has homie popped any questions your way yet?"

Emily shook her head. "Not yet," she admitted, teetering between wondering when he would and whether he'd take it back once he knew.

Benny found a maroon T-shirt and pulled it over his head. "Has he come out and said the L-word?"

She shrugged. "Not in so many words. He sure treats me like he does."

"Yeah? How?" Wade asked as he pulled on a sock.

"The morning after Chucky beat him to a pulp he sat beside my hospital bed instead of curling up in his own. He brings me coffee in bed in the morning. Gifts me with pretty things he knows I'll like, like this pearl choker."

"That pretty pearl choker set him back a small fortune. I saw the receipt," Benny piped up.

"Aw, he can afford it. He's raking in the money at Blakely," Wade scoffed.

"You don't know how proud that makes me," she said. "So back to your question…no, he hasn't come out and said he loves me, but his actions would certainly say that he does. Besides, he's practically let me design the new house for him. Why would he do that if he didn't plan to share it with me?"

"Because he has lousy taste and knows it?" She shot Wade the finger. He grinned. "I agree. Those are definitely the actions of a man who's in love, way in love."

"So now he needs to pop the question," Benny said. "Want us to drop a hint his way?"

"Lord God, no," she said, half amused and half terrified. "He'll ask me when he's good and ready." She flopped down on the sofa. "I just wish he'd hurry up. I'd like to get his formal proposal so I could tell him the truth."

"I don't get why you don't go ahead and tell him," Benny said. "He's going to find out sooner or later. Why not sooner? Do I have any clean socks in the clothes?"

"You know why." Emily rooted around and found two socks that more or less matched and threw them toward Benny. "I want to be sure, damned sure of his reasons for being with me."

"I'm probably going to get cursed at for saying this, but if you don't trust Jason to love you for yourself you probably don't have any business marrying him," Benny observed.

"That's just it, Benny. How the hell do I know I can trust him after what happened before?" Emily snapped. "And it happened not once, but twice."

"Emily's right to be cautious," Wade said. "Sure, Jason seems like a really wonderful guy and I personally would be very surprised if he gave a damn one way or the other. On the other hand, all he's been able to talk about since he got that job is how well he's doing and how damn much money he's bringing home."

"I know that and, God forgive me, even though I'm proud of him it's getting a little irritating. And that's why I'm worried," she said. "It does seem awfully important to him." Way more important to him than she wished it was.

"Maybe it's just his way of compensating for the scarring and the fact that he's thirty years old and just now has his degree and his life back to the point that he can even enter the work force," Benny argued. "You can't really compare him to Jeff Carmichaels or Brandon Bentley."

"Jeff wasn't so bad, not really," she murmured. "He was just doing what his family expected him to do."

"Wuss," Wade spat out.

"Kind of." Emily agreed. "Jeff grew up in the same Alamo Heights enclave I did. Family alliances are as common as two-carat diamonds in that neighborhood. Happens all the time. Eventually, Jeff and I finally looked at one another and realized expectations weren't enough for us to build a life together. Last I heard he's dating a socialite from Houston and they're doing fine. His family will be pleased with his choice. They always made it clear to Jeff what their expectations are in terms of a wife."

"Sounds kind of cold if you ask me," Wade sneered.

"It is. But some of them work anyway."

"And I'll bet a lot of those nice folks have all kinds of stuff on the side with people they really care about," Benny said. He sat down and pulled on a Red Wing boot.

"That they do," Emily laughed.

"What about your family? What about their expectations?" Wade asked curiously.

Emily paused. "Five generations' worth. Success is a foregone conclusion, as is taking one's place in the community. Granddad's having apoplexy about my generation. Especially Russ, not going to work for the family firm."

"Do they still expect you to make one of those family alliances after the first one went sour on you?" Wade persisted.

"Maybe not so much with the marriage business—my parents and my grandparents married for love. Besides, it wasn't Jeff that left such a sour taste in my mouth; it was Brandon." Her eyes clouded. "I thought I really loved that bastard." She stopped and took a deep breath. "And you know the worst part of finding him in bed with that drop-dead beautiful bitch? Him telling me how ugly he thinks I am."

"You're not ugly, Emily," Benny said quickly.

"I'm no beauty, either. My face is as round as an apple and I have red hair from hell."

"So what if you're not a supermodel? Doesn't mean much in the course of things. My mom's as pretty as they come and she's been through hell in her life." Wade shrugged. "If you want to wait until you're sure of Jason, then go ahead and wait. It's not going to hurt anything if he doesn't find out until after you have his ring on your finger."

Benny's brow came together. "I'd be pissed and so will Jason when he finds out. But we'll keep our traps shut if that's what you want, Em."

"Thanks, guys. Let me get Jason out of the shower and grease him down and we'll be out in a couple of minutes."

Was Benny right? Was Jason going to be angry when he found out? Would telling him everything at this point be worse when she wasn't completely sure why he was with her?

As she walked into her apartment, she heard the water go off and stepped into the bathroom as the squeaky shower door opened. She licked her lips as Jason toweled off the excess water. *Gawd*, that man's body. Grabbing his big bottle of the special moisturizing lotion designed for burn scars, she asked, "Back or front first?"

"Doesn't matter," Jason said as he dipped his face for a kiss, nipping and nibbling, bringing her nipples to hard points.

"Cut that out," she breathed, reluctantly taking a step back. "You keep that up and we'll never get out of here." She poured a small puddle of lotion in the palm of her hand. "Now let me do my job."

Slowly, starting in the middle of Jason's horribly scarred chest, she applied the lotion gently and lovingly. Careful of the areas still bruised and tender from Chucky's beating, she worked in enough to moisturize the damaged flesh, careful not to miss any spots as she covered his chest. Adding more lotion, she moved lower, grinning when the circle she made on his stomach caused him to flinch and his thick penis to jump against her fingers.

"Damn, you're killing me, woman," he breathed as she mischievously let her hand drift lower to caress his hard shaft. "You better quit that or we really won't get out of here tonight."

"Poor Jason," she teased. She took his hand and poured in a generous dollop. "Get your face and head while I get your legs."

Jason obligingly put the lotion on his face, head and neck while Emily crouched down and applied the moisturizer to the scars on his muscular legs. She attended to the lesser scars on his back where the doctors had harvested skin for grafting and gave his hard firm butt a little massage just for the fun of it.

"Em-il-ee," Jason warned. She grinned and let her hands cup his sculpted ass. "Oh, hell, woman," he laughed as she snaked her arms around his body and stroked her hand down his long penis. "What are you doing?"

She made a production of stepping back and throwing her hands into the air. "Just giving you something to think about tonight while we're out," she said wickedly. "Now get your clothes on while I check my sugar and take my insulin. Benny and Wade are waiting."

Emily was pleased that her blood sugar was a little better. She made quick work of the insulin and found Jason in the bedroom dressed in a pair of tight jeans and a long-sleeved T-shirt. Her lips thinned. It would probably be hot in the bar, but she shrugged inwardly. If he wanted to wear the long-sleeved shirt tonight then so be it. But she pointed and shook her head when he added a ball cap to his ensemble. "There's no sun where we're going and it clashes with the shirt. Lose it."

Jason threw the offending cap on the coffee table. "Anything for my lady." He reached out and touched the end of her still-beaded nipple gently with his finger. "I love that I can turn you on."

Emily took his hand and laid it against her cheek. "And if you think I'm turned on now, just wait until I get you in that bed tonight." She tilted her head, reached up and pulled Jason's lips to hers. "Baby, you turn me on soooo much."

* * *

God, I hope so, Jason thought as he captured Emily's lips in a hard, passionate, bone-crushing kiss that rocked him to his toes. *I hope I turn her on the way that she does me.* He still couldn't quite believe that this young, vibrant, wonderful woman had come into his life— elbowed her way in, actually, past his resentment and his bitterness and the crippling embarrassment with which he faced the world, and convinced him that he could come out of the shadows and live life to the fullest again.

She was the first, and perhaps the only woman since that horrible afternoon in Iraq, who had been willing or able to look past the scars and the disfigurement to find the real him. The man that had been buried after his world had been turned upside down, who had endured months of agony and years of surgeries while the doctors pieced together a new body covering for him. God love her, she accepted him, completely accepted him, for who he was now.

She had worked her magic and given him the courage to keep looking for a job when it seemed hopeless; she had enlisted her sister Holly, another wounded veteran, to plead his case with the man who eventually hired him. It amazed him, truly, to feel her body heat and her nipples tighten and know that in spite of the way he looked, he turned her on just as much as she did him.

It was a miracle, really, that he could make her feel the way she did.

Jason feasted greedily at Emily's eager lips, breaking off their kiss only when he heard loud banging on the front door. "You guys coming or are we leaving without you?" his erstwhile roommate Wade yelled through the window.

Jason raised his head and grinned down at the now-flustered Emily. "Eat your hearts out, fellas," he said as he placed one more light kiss on her lips. "Lip gloss. Smeared," he whispered, proud of his accomplishment then laughed when Emily beat a hasty retreat to fix her makeup.

The four of them piled into Jason's latest demo. "So it's meet-the-parents weekend?" Benny asked as Jason backed out of the driveway. "Nervous? Excited? Rather run in the other direction?"

"Yes, yes, and not really," Jason laughed.

"And you get to meet the grandparents, too, I guess." Benny laughed wickedly. "I hear Granddaddy's the real ring-tailed tooter."

Emily rolled her eyes. "Who's been talking about Granddad?"

"Russ told Rory a little about him. Apparently he eats grandchildren for breakfast."

Emily laughed. "Only if we don't go to law school and join the family firm, which come to think of it most of us didn't. But I don't think Jason has any reason to be nervous about anything."

"Emily's probably right," Jason said. "Besides, I've already met Mr. and Mrs. Riley."

"So you're not nervous then," Benny said. "Not if you've already met them."

"Didn't say that. Let's just say I can tell Mr. Riley has reservations about me and that I'm hoping to lay a few of them to rest this weekend."

"What reservations?" Emily demanded. "They were perfectly nice to you all three times they were around you."

"Yes, they were, and your mother couldn't have been more warm and accepting. But let's just say the salesman in me can tell I haven't quite closed the deal yet with your father, and I hope to do that this weekend."

"And you might get that started by not talking quite so much about your job so much," Emily murmured to no one in particular. "And all the money you're raking in."

"Uh-oh, did our friend Jason here lay it on a little too thick?" Wade asked.

"With a trowel, you mean?" Emily teased.

Jason felt a stab of irritation that he didn't try to hide. "I was trying to let on to your parents that I am doing well at the new job. After all, I didn't even have a job when I met them back in the summer. Now I have a decent job and am making a little something and I wanted them to know it. I just don't want them to think you're dating a loser." Jason glanced in the rearview mirror and wondered at the look Benny and Wade exchanged.

"Jason, they don't think you're a loser," Emily said as she reached out and squeezed his arm. "And the only reason I didn't kick you under the table that night is that I am proud of how well you're doing. Damn proud, and if you wanted to toot your own horn a little it sure didn't bother me. But maybe in the future you might soft-pedal it a little."

"I can do that," he acquiesced. "So guys, plan to do any deer hunting over Thanksgiving weekend?"

Jason listened with half an ear as Wade and Benny regaled Emily with stories of their hunting exploits, but his mind drifted back to their earlier discussion. Yes, financial success was important to him. Damned important. Although Emily would probably not approve of or appreciate the importance it held to him.

His parents were doing well now, but their financial success had happened only in the last five years or so, and Jason had grown up in a household where every penny was pinched, accounted for, and pinched again. He'd had to take out loans and work night jobs to pay for his first years of college, and even now everything he had was something he'd earned for himself.

But the real moment that his financial success had started to matter, really matter, was the moment he realized he'd fallen head over heels in love with Emily Riley. It was for her that he wanted to make a success of himself so badly. Although he liked nice things as much as the next man, it wasn't for himself that he wanted to make a good living and build a nice house and fashion a comfortable life. He wanted to do it for Emily. He wanted to give that nice life to her.

Jason glanced up in the rearview mirror and caught a glimpse of his virtually obliterated face and the mass of scars that had taken its place. He winced inwardly as he always did when he had to look at the physical destruction that was now Jason Edward Donahue. Damn it, looking like he did, he better be able to offer Emily something besides just an ugly mug, a body still suffering the aftereffects of having over half its skin burned off, and all that entailed. And when he factored in the lung damage caused by the hot gases and fumes from the explosives, he knew she wasn't getting any kind of physical prize in him.

Jason's lips tightened as a couple of good-looking young men on the sidewalk spotted Emily. Their faces split into wide grins and they whistled and waved to get her attention. Damn, they were cocky little bastards, he thought when she whistled and waved back. Young and so damned handsome; secure in who they were and what they had to offer. Those were words and feelings that no longer applied to him in any way, shape or form.

'Cute' and 'handsome' had gone by the wayside the day of the explosion in Baghdad. 'Young' had disappeared a day at a time during the years of surgeries, rehabilitation, additional surgeries, additional rehabilitation, and eventual return to college while his twenties disappeared. He dropped further and further behind his contemporaries, who had gotten degrees, married, and started careers and families. And 'secure' in what he had to offer? That was the biggest joke of all.

Sweet, optimistic Emily—she honestly thought he was getting over the self-consciousness about his appearance. Yeah, he was coping with it and his success at work had helped, but, in some ways, it was worse than before, especially when he was in public with Emily. Strangers stared, their expressions clearly wondering why she would be with a man who looked like he did, or they took pity that she had no choice but to be with him.

So hell yeah, he was insecure. Sorry ass that he was, he hadn't even been able to get up the courage to tell the woman he loved how he felt about her—or to ask her to marry him. He'd had his grandmother's ring for almost a month now, and it was still buried in the dresser under what few things were in the bedroom at Wade and Benny's place.

He glanced in the rearview at Emily's fans. No, he didn't have their looks, their vitality, their youth, or their optimism, but he'd offer her a comfortable life and the house of her dreams. He'd give it another month or two to show her and her family that he could offer her a lifestyle most women dreamed about.

If he was fortunate enough to get her to agree to marry him, he would make damned sure he gave her the good life, and with luck, that might make up for not being to offer her much of anything else.

Chapter Three

Emily smiled as she took Jason's hand when they stepped into what was probably her favorite bar in the world. Unpretentious, with lots of dark, carved-up wood, the lingering odor of old beer had seeped into the floor, and the walls still smelled faintly of cigarettes years after a no-smoking ban had gone into effect. Generations of Aggies had eaten burgers and consumed beer in the not-quite-a-dive, and, ever since a student in the 1970s had accidentally dropped his senior ring in a pitcher of Shiner Bock then chugged the pitcher to retrieve the ring, Aggies had been 'dunking' their rings with gusto.

Although still early in the evening, the bar was almost full and there was an atmosphere of celebration in the air. It was only the twenty that Jason slipped the hostess that got the four of them a small table close to the back. Wade and Benny looked around and spotted a couple of juniors, Gina and Mary Lynn from two duplexes over.

"Ladies, we're about to embark upon the time-honored ritual of dunking our bright and shiny A&M senior rings," Wade said, waving them over. "Want to join the festivities?"

The girls nodded eagerly, picked up their chairs to carry them over to the already-crowded table. "Thanks, Wade," Gina said, fluttering her eyelashes a little at the handsome young man.

"Yeah, thank you. Our girls' night out was falling kind of flat," Mary Lynn said. "We've been sitting there for thirty whole minutes and not one guy's come up and offered to buy us a beer. Everybody's just here to do their rings. Doesn't anybody want to get laid tonight?"

And just how many of those beers has Mary Lynn already consumed? Emily looked over at Jason, both of them fighting not to laugh out loud. "Isn't the point of a girls' night out to spend time with your girlfriends?" Emily asked innocently.

Mary Lynn shook her head. "Not now that we're twenty-one."

All three guys laughed out loud. Emily wasn't sure what turning twenty-one had to do with it; the waitress arrived to take their order before she could ask. The savvy server spotted the three brand-new senior rings and Jason's slightly older one. "Three dunkings or four?" she asked as she held her pencil over her order ticket.

"None for me, we dunked mine awhile back," Jason said.

"Just two, actually," Emily said. She gestured to Wade and Benny. "For them."

"Like hell," Wade said. "You're going to dunk just like we are." He turned to the waitress. "Bring her a pitcher of unsweetened tea. She can dunk hers with that."

"I'll be happy to," the waitress said. "But y'all do know that some jake-leg passed an ordinance that we can only bring you a thirty-two ounce mug to dunk with these days, right? No pitchers."

"We'd heard something to that effect, but were hoping you'd maybe bend the rules a little tonight," Benny wiggled his eyebrows.

"Sorry, no can do. A&M students have the highest rate of metallic foreign body ingestion of any college in the United States," she said sweetly.

"Okay, beer for the guys, tea for Emily." Jason looked around the table. "Burgers for everybody okay?" They all nodded. "Tonight's on me."

The waitress disappeared and Gina turned to Jason. She started to flirt with him but finally took a good look at him and lowered her eyes instead. "Thank you for your hospitality," she said politely. "Aren't you Wade and Benny's roommate?"

"Not too often anymore," Wade said. "He's with her," dipping his head toward Emily.

Gina was momentarily taken aback but hid it quickly. "I didn't realize the two of you were an item."

"Yep, since summer," Jason murmured. "She's taken pity on this ugly mug of mine."

"What happened?" Gina asked. "The war?"

"Iraq. I was one of the unlucky ones, I guess."

"You're not all that unlucky in my book," Mary Lynn said tartly. "You lived, didn't you? My big brother came home in a body bag."

Wade and Benny's eyes widened and Emily could feel Jason flinch next to her. "Well, hell, that sucks," Wade murmured.

"I am so sorry for your loss," Emily added.

Jason reached over and touched Mary Lynn gently on her hand. "You hit the nail on the head. I *am* one of the lucky ones. Thank you for the reminder."

"So are you still in school?" Gina asked quickly.

"No, I have my degree and am cutting a wide swath at Blakeley Chevrolet." Emily shot Jason a look, which he promptly ignored. "Doing great if I do say so myself."

Emily breathed a sigh of relief when Jason and Mary Lynn went on to discuss the business department faculty. Damn, she knew Jason was proud of how well he was doing, but did he have to bring it up every time he turned around? Was that all he thought about? Money? Emily bit her lip. She couldn't help but wonder how he was going to react when she told him her little secret.

The burgers arrived a few minutes later, along with two big mugs of beer for Wade and Benny and a third mug for Emily filled to the brim with cold tea without the ice. "We've never done one with tea before, but I figured you'd want to get the entire experience," the waitress laughed. "Why the tea?"

"Diabetic," Emily murmured as she eyed the tea doubtfully. "I have to drink the whole thing in one gulp?"

"Yes!" the entire table said in unison.

"Fine, but I'm not going first. Wade, you're on."

Wade twisted off his senior ring and threw it in the mug. "Okay, here goes." He picked up the mug, put it to his lips, and started gulping down the beer in huge swallows. He continued swallowing the beer long after Emily was convinced she would have been gagging, and sure enough he finished the last swallow and tipped over the mug to get his ring.

"Way to go, Wade," Gina crowed as Wade let out with a belch that could be heard all over the bar. The other patrons of the bar clapped and whistled as Wade wiped his ring on a napkin and returned it to his finger.

Emily and Benny looked at one another. "My mama always said that ladies should go first," he said slyly.

Emily looked around the table. They were all eyeing her expectantly and Jason looked like he was about to laugh out loud.

May as well get it over with. She tugged off her senior ring and tossed it in the tea then picked up the tea and put it to her lips.

God, am I ever going to get to the bottom of this mug? Emily swallowed and tried to take a breath. How in the hell had Russ and Holly ever finished off a whole pitcher? She gulped down a few swallows, praying she was getting close to the bottom then breathed a sigh of relief when she felt the cold metal of her ring against her lips. Forcing herself not to gag, she retrieved her ring, set the mug on the table and took a bow as the bar patrons clapped and whistled for her, too.

Benny made quick work of his mug, prompting Jason to comment that Benny drank all his beer like that, and they tackled the burgers with gusto. As they finished, Emily started to feel the effects of all the tea and excused herself to go to the restroom.

Easing her way through the exit hallway full of other dunkers circling the facilities, she bumped into a young man just coming out of the men's room. She backed away then looked up to apologize and instead found herself smiling into the dark, handsome face of Buddy Rodriguez, her lab partner in advanced microbiology. Buddy looked down and his face broke into a wide grin.

"So what brings you here tonight?"

Emily held up her ring. "What else? You, too?"

"Naw, don't get mine 'til next year. Had too much fun a couple of years back and lost almost a semester's worth of credit." He moved closer, placing his arm against the wall, effectively trapping her in the hallway. "Say, how about I buy you another beer to celebrate?"

"I'll pass," she said. "I'm with friends tonight. See you next week in lab."

Emily ducked under his arm and headed for their table, surprised that Buddy had come on to her since he'd never shown any interest before. She didn't realize he had followed her through the crowded bar back to her table until she sat down and he slid into the seat that Gina had vacated during Emily's absence.

"I'd still like to buy you that beer," Buddy said as he looked around the table, flinching a bit when his eyes landed on Jason.

"Actually, I don't drink beer," she said quickly, sliding her hand into Jason's. "Jason, I'd like you to meet my lab partner from advanced micro this semester. Buddy Rodriguez, my boyfriend,

Jason Donahue." Dipping her head in each person's direction, she continued, "Mary Lynn, Wade and Benny."

Buddy shook hands all around. Pointedly, she left her hand in Jason's, but rather than take her obvious hint, Buddy sat down beside her as close as the chairs would allow then commenced flirting outrageously. At first Jason seemed amused, but after several minutes, when Buddy showed no signs of letting up, she could feel Jason's amusement turning to irritation.

She tried to signal Wade and Benny to do something, anything to distract Buddy, but they were more interested in ordering another beer. Wade finally caught the eye of their server

"Anybody else want anything?" the waitress chirped as Jason handed over his credit card.

Mary Lynn said, "Another beer for me and more tea for Emily." Jason looked at Buddy. "Can I get you anything?"

"Sure, I'll have a Corona," Buddy said. "And thanks. I'm mostly running on empty right now."

"Not a problem." Jason smiled enigmatically. "I remember what it was like to be running on empty."

And it wasn't all that long ago, was it? Emily thought dryly.

"You're not broke like the rest of us?" Buddy laughed.

"Nope, he's doing great. He said so earlier." Mary Lynn swallowed the rest of her beer.

"Really?" Buddy asked. "Doing what, if you don't mind my asking?"

"Car sales," Jason said proudly. "Number one salesman last month and the month before that."

Here we go again.

Jason went on to talk about the nice demo he drove and the house plans he was working on. The more Jason expounded on his accomplishments the more Emily worried; his focus on money might be more critical to their future than she had allowed. Perhaps ruining the chance at a future.

Interestingly, Jason's boasting had the desired effect, and after drinking his beer rather quickly, Buddy wished them all a good evening and left their table.

Emily turned, exasperated, to Jason. "Did you absolutely have to do that?" she hissed through gritted teeth.

"Do what?" Jason asked innocently. "Pay for his beer?"

Wade and Benny looked at one another and laughed out loud. "Well, that's one way to get rid of the competition. Tell us; is your dick bigger than his, too?" Benny laughed.

"Slick, Jason. And you didn't even have to throw a punch like Tommy Joe Reece did," Wade added.

Jason looked puzzled. "I thought Tommy Joe is in a wheel chair."

"He is," Wade and Benny said in unison. Benny went on. "That didn't stop him from decking the clown hitting on Christi."

Emily looked at the three of them and shook her head. Clearly this was a guy thing, "What. Ever," she valley-girled. "I don't know about you, but I'm about ready to call it a night."

Mary Lynn refused their offer of a ride and soon they were headed back to the duplex. Emily wished Wade and Benny a safe trip to Verde and followed Jason into their side of the building.

"I thought you were going to soft-pedal the horn-tooting from now on," Emily complained as she sat on the bed and pulled off her boots. "Instead, not only did you brag to those girls, you made a complete ass of yourself in front of Buddy."

Jason kicked off his shoes and pulled his shirt over his head. "How else was I going to get rid of him? Would you prefer I deck him like Tommy Joe? Remember, I don't have the wheelchair sympathy routine going on to keep me from getting arrested. I'm just ugly."

"Jason, that's just mean," Emily said. "Damn it, I'd made it clear that you're my boyfriend and that I was there with you."

"And he was respecting that so much, now wasn't he?" He didn't wait for an answer. "No, he was laying in on so thick we could've planted corn in it. I used the most effective weapon at my disposal to discourage him from continuing to hit on you. Worked, didn't it?"

"But why did it have to be a money thing? Why does it always have to be a money thing? Is somebody's bank account always the most important thing about them?"

Jason stopped, thought for a moment then lifted a shoulder. "Not always, but at times it sure as hell can be." He shed all but his boxers. "I'm hungry again. You want anything?" dropping the conversation as if it didn't matter, or worse, making it a foregone conclusion.

She shook her head then sucked in a deep breath as Jason disappeared into the kitchen. Well, he couldn't have made his feelings much plainer, could he? He did think money was important—quantum important.

Emily dropped her head into her hands. If she'd had any doubts about not telling Jason her secret, those doubts just sailed out the door. His feelings about her would definitely be influenced if he knew she was a wealthy trust-fund baby.

Clearly, it would make a huge difference if he knew about her money. She couldn't tell him. She absolutely *would not* tell him about the money until she had a ring on her finger; otherwise she'd spend the rest of her life wondering just what it was about her that he really loved—her, or her bank balance.

Stripping off her clothes, she pulled a cotton sleep shirt over her head then turned back the covers, but a faint rumbling in her stomach hinted that in spite of the burger, she just might be hungry after all. Another check of her sugar level sealed the deal and she went off to the kitchen, where she found Jason sitting in front of an almost-empty bowl of cornflakes.

She got a bowl and he pushed the cornflakes and the milk across the table. "Still pissed?" he asked as she dug into her cereal.

"Yep," she nodded. "You weren't going to brag about the job anymore, remember?"

Jason put down his spoon and stared at her across the table. "Sorry you were embarrassed," he said derisively. "I just wanted to get rid of that little bastard. He threatened me."

Emily's spoon stopped halfway to her mouth. "How did he threaten *you*? He didn't say a word to you. It was me he was trying to hit on."

"You have to ask that? Jesus, he took one look at me and completely dismissed me. Never mind that I was sitting there holding your hand; he simply would not respect the fact that you were there with me. No, he tried to hit on the disfigured dude's lady because, you know what? The ugly guy simply doesn't matter. And Gina was no better. She was flat-out shocked that you were even with me." He picked up his bowl and drank the rest of his milk. "It gets old, Em. Being dismissed cuz of the way I look. So I fought back with the only weapon I have. They didn't respect the face, so I gave them something they could respect." He stood up and put the table and distance between them. "It bothers the hell out of me when a good-looking bastard like Buddy Rodriguez hits on you. I try not to be jealous, but, well, you're so beautiful and all…"

Emily laughed ruefully. "Jason, I am not beautiful. I am not even pretty. Far from it, in fact, and you know it."

"Don't say that," he growled. "You are beautiful, and I know good-looking guys are going to hit on you; I just wish I could compete…"

She was on the move when he growled. The rest of his thought got swallowed up by her hungry kiss. She wound her arms around his middle and held him tightly against her body, forcing him feel the stiff points of her nipples as they dug into his tender skin.

She snaked her tongue into his mouth, finding his and engaging it in a fierce duel. For the first few seconds he let her kiss him, but as her body called out to his, he edged even closer, cradling her head gently but firmly as he took over, claiming her as she came alive in his arms.

For long moments they clung to each other, his tight muscles and swelling cock relaying a sensual invitation that she longed to answer as she dampened with need.

After long moments, he raised his head. "Does that feel like you're not beautiful?"

Emily breathed. "Does that feel like you can't compete? Like you have to worry about all those other guys? What can I do to make you understand I want you and only you?"

Jason grinned wickedly. "Well, maybe for starters you could kiss me like that again." He tilted her face toward his and kissed her, this kiss under his sensuous control from the start. She let him take the lead, returning his passion with more of her own.

How could he not know? How could he not understand just how much she desired him? She didn't give a damn about his scars. Hell, when she looked at him she didn't see the scars, she saw *him*. Why didn't he get that?

Eventually, Jason pulled back and leaned his forehead against hers. "Wanna take this to a nice, comfortable horizontal setting?"

"Sure, if we can find one somewhere." She laughed as Jason whisked her into his arms and carried her to the lumpy old double bed in the only bedroom of their half of the duplex.

He dumped her down in the middle of the bed and lay down beside her. "The first thing I'm going to buy when I get that house built is a California King with a pillow-top mattress, and we are going to spend at least twenty-four hours breaking it in." He cradled her against his chest. "You know you're precious to me, right?" He ran his hand down the side of her face and nibbled her lips. "So beautiful. So precious. Such a gift." She could feel him swelling even harder. "God, the way you turn me on, sometimes I just can't believe it."

"Believe it. Oh, believe it," she breathed as she bent her head and deepened the kiss.

Easing the night-shirt over her head, he asked, "Why aren't you wearing that sexy black thing?" He bent his head and brushed his lips over her now-naked breast.

"I packed it just in case," she laughed. "I know—wishful thinking." She arched her breast toward his eager lips. "Besides, wouldn't you rather have me naked?"

"Naked works." Jason suckled her nipple until it was a sharp peak in his mouth.

"So if naked works, let's get you just as naked."

He reached down and unceremoniously jerked the silk boxers from his body while she unabashedly took in the sight of his magnificent erection. There must be a God and He must be merciful, Emily thought, because of all the burns he suffered, Jason's genital area was untouched, and his long, throbbing penis, thrusting outward from a nest of light brown hair, stood at stiff attention and ready for her loving ministrations.

She paid his swollen cock her most careful attention, stroking down the thick shaft, reaching around and cupping his balls in her fingers and gently caressing them the way he loved. He reveled in the sensation for a moment or two, laying on his back and letting her work her erotic magic, before rolling over and trapping her beneath his long, hard body.

"That feels great, but if you don't stop I'm not going to last until the main event."

"Oh, my, can't have that," she teased as he trailed a path of kisses down her body, starting with her breasts, teasing first one and then the other. Her legs shifted restlessly as his lips travel lower, slowly kissing a path to first her navel, where he tickled her until she was squirming beneath him, and then lower still, slowly approaching her patch of fiery red hair.

Jason shifted on the bed and grasped her knees. "Open up for me, Em. Let me see you." Shyly, she opened her legs. "Still not used to me being down here, are you?" Jason teased as he pushed her legs even farther apart, leaving her exposed and vulnerable.

"It's just… nobody else ever…" Jason's tongue snaked out and Emily nearly came off the bed as he touched and stroked her at her core.

How the hell does he do that? she wondered, not for the first time, as he wrapped his almost prehensile tongue around her, bathing her in the delicious sensation of its slightly roughened surface.

Tension grew tighter and tighter until her entire body exploded in delight, shivers of pleasure shooting from her tight center to the top of her head and the tips of her fingers and toes. For long moments the tremors shook her, sweeping her into the maelstrom of pleasure she always felt with Jason.

She lay still for a moment while she caught her breath. "That was amazing."

Jason slid up her body and positioned himself over her. "With us it's always amazing." He kissed her ear as he eased his length into her sensitive channel. "Thanks for getting the IUD," he whispered as her gave her body a moment to adjust to his presence. "Just you and me with nothing in between, that's what's amazing."

Emily thrust her hips toward his when he began to move within her. Slowly at first as they both adjusted to the rhythm he set then, as the excitement and pressure grew, he moved faster and faster, building the tension within them as they spiraled together toward the explosive conclusion that was coming.

Her body arched as the climactic moment hit, gasping and calling out his name as another earth-shaking orgasm tore through her body. Triggered by her release, Jason stiffened above her, hoarsely calling out her name as his seed shot deep into her body.

Without breaking their connection, he rolled to one side, bringing her up so that they faced one another. Pushing her damp hair away from her flushed face, he stared into her eyes. "Good?" he asked softly as she settled her arm around his waist.

"Ummmm. But then, it always is." She felt his overheated chest. "Do you need to get into a cool shower?"

Jason shook his head and laughed. "Isn't that what I'm supposed to do if I *don't* get to have you? No, honey, I'm fine. I'll cool down in a minute." He leaned forward for a long lingering kiss and she could feel him again start to swell inside of her. "Or maybe no," he said against her lips. "Maybe I'll stay hot for a while longer."

"That works, too," she mumbled as she returned his kisses.

He rolled over on his back, taking Emily with him so that she sat astride his hips, impaled on him like a pagan goddess. Her body arched above him, her hair a bright fiery halo cascading down around her neck and shoulders, her breasts and berry-bright nipples bouncing just out of reach of his eager lips.

He reached up and covered her breasts with his large scarred hands, her tight little nipples digging into his palms. "Can you feel them?" Emily asked wickedly. "Can you feel how turned on I am already?"

Jason nodded and rubbed circles on her breasts as Emily bounced above him. It was slower this time and more relaxed, yet it wasn't too long before they were crying out again as a long, simultaneous orgasm overcame them both.

Spent, she rolled off of him, breaking their intimate contact to snuggle down beside him. "Two orgasms in thirty minutes and if we didn't have to get up in the morning you could probably get a couple more out of me." She placed a sweet kiss on the side of his chest. "Still worried that you don't turn me on?"

Instead of the grin she was expecting, Jason looked at her with an expression that was almost pensive. "I don't think so. At least not right now." And then he did grin. "But you're welcome to reassure me any time you feel like it."

"Cheeky." She threw her arm over his chest. "Want your boxers?"

"Nah. Want your night shirt?"

"Nah." She snuggled down beside him in the crook of his arm.

* * *

Thirty minutes later as she stared into the darkened bedroom, she replayed their great romp. Okay, two romps. But neither had solved a single one of the issues that plagued them.

Jason had drifted off to sleep, his breathing even and relaxed, and normally she would have joined him in slumber long ago. But her mind kept drifting back over the events of the day, robbing her of her peace and chasing the sleep from her bed.

She was lying to Jason, lying by omission perhaps, but lying just the same. But how could she tell him the truth after he'd come out and said that sometimes someone's bank account was the most important thing about them? How could she come out and tell him that she was the product of five generations of wealth and privilege and expectations? How was he going to feel when he learned that the financial success he was so proud of was not celebrated in her family—it was the expected norm and God help you if you didn't pony up? –What if she told him about her generous trust fund and it became the most important thing about her? Would she ever know if he loved her for herself?

And could she ever help him overcome his insecurity about the scarring? It hadn't been just pride about his income tonight that made him boast; he had been genuinely insecure when Buddy came on to her.

And that bothered her down to her boots.

She'd spent the last five months trying to convince him that he— Jason Donahue—appealed to her, and that she loved him and wanted him, scars or no scars. It seemed that she was not succeeding and she didn't have a clue what she could do differently, particularly if their great sex couldn't make him see how she felt.

Tears welled up in her eyes. God, she loved this man.

She eased out from under Jason's arm, careful not to wake him, and sat up on the side of the bed where she could reach the box of tissues. She loved him so much, and she thought he loved her. But there were some real issues between them, issues that they were going to have to resolve soon before they could count on a life together.

She was very aware of that.

And, she thought, so was Jason.

Chapter Four

Jason pulled on his ball cap and pushed the Open button to the car's sunroof. The sun shone brightly and felt good even through the protective long-sleeved outer shirt and cap he had to wear.

"Wow, that feels great," he shouted over the sound of air whistling into the car. The cool breeze was perfumed by the delicious aroma of the huge Bastrop pine trees that were re-growing after the devastating wildfire that had decimated most of the forest a few years back.

Emily put on her sunglasses and pulled her hair into a ponytail. "Yep, feels wonderful. Want your sunglasses?"

Jason nodded as she wiped the lenses then handed them over. "So how does it feel to be going back to San Antonio? After all that time in SAMMC, do you hate the place?"

"San Antonio or SAMMC?"

"Either, I guess."

Jason thought a minute. "San Antonio, not at all. I used to go down there with Mom and Dad all the time when I was a kid. I love the zoo, and the Riverwalk is something else. But SAMMC – the military hospital? I realize they worked a miracle on me there, but if I never go back again as long as I live it won't break my heart any. Some of the most miserable days of my life were spent in that place."

"Holly's not wild about it either, and I think Tommy Joe Reece refers to it as the Shiny White House of Horrors. How long were you there?"

"Three years," Jason said tersely. "On and off."

He saw the shudder work its way through her. Surely, she was imagining the horror of surgeries and rehab that went on for three years of his life.

"We'll find you some more fun places to hang out." She reached out and took his hand. "They did work a miracle, you know."

Something he needed to remind himself of more often, he thought as he recalled Mary Lynn's comment about her fallen brother. Jason gunned the engine and they roared down the state highway.

He drank in the sight of Emily Riley in the passenger seat beside him, her hair blowing wildly in spite of the ponytail and the freckles on her nose getting darker in the sun. Yes, they still had some issues to work through, and they would; then he'd give her the best and brightest future a woman could ever hope for. He had to give her that, he thought as he glanced in the rearview mirror and caught a momentary glimpse of his face, still noticeably disfigured even behind the ball cap and sunglasses. He had to give her a reason to ignore the young, cute guys when they made a pass at her. He had to give her a reason to put up with the stares and the shudders and the looks of horror that came her way when she was with him. He had to give her a reason to grease him down every morning and evening and look at his ugly damned face first thing after waking up. He had to give her a reason to want to stay with him, or one of these days she was going to take a look at him and decide he wasn't worth the staying.

They made good time until they reached I-35, where they found themselves bumper to bumper pretty much all the way in to San Antonio. He offered to stop at the malls outside San Marcos, but Emily took one look at the crowded parking lot and decided to postpone her retail therapy for another time.

Jason asked her to enter her parent's address in the GPS and, completely absorbed in negotiating his way through the heavy traffic both on the interstate and the city streets, he paid no attention to where the machine was sending them until he turned onto Broadway, the major thoroughfare through the tony old neighborhood of Alamo Heights. He glanced over at the GPS and felt his eyes widen. She had entered an address in the heart of the wealthiest old-money neighborhood in San Antonio. *What in the hell was going on?* He looked over at Emily, who appeared unconcerned at the direction they were heading.

"Uh, is this where we're supposed to be going?"

"Uh-huh. The house is just a couple of blocks from here. And there's the elementary school I went to when I was little."

He spared a glance at the old, but scrupulously maintained little school while he tried to wrap his mind around this turn of events. Sure, he knew she didn't come from poverty; her dad was an attorney and the family owned a modest lake house in Heaven's Point. But her mother didn't bring in a second income and Emily certainly didn't live extravagantly like some of the other A&M students; she wore jeans and T-shirts and lived in a run-down duplex and drove a three-year-old Mazda. He had expected a four-bedroom ranch or a nice two-story in an affluent suburb, not an address in a neighborhood that positively reeked of old money—and a lot of it.

The GPS sent them on one more turn and placed them at a large stone house surrounded by a rock fence topped with lacy iron work. The sprawling, beautifully groomed front yard was chock full of towering oak and pecan trees and a circular driveway curved around to the double front doors.

Jason forced himself not to gawk at the lovely old home and his mind raced as he tried for an explanation. How could a lawyer, even a good lawyer with a prestigious firm, afford something like this? Jason itched to ask Emily how her parents managed to buy this place, but he determinedly put a clamp on his curiosity. He would be damned if he asked a question like that. It was none of his business, and he wasn't sure he even wanted to know. Besides, it didn't necessarily have anything to do with Emily anyway. Just because her parents had managed to afford this place, it didn't mean she had money, too. If she had, she surely would have mentioned it at some point.

He sneaked a glance over at her. Good God Almighty. Why hadn't she bothered to mention she came from the richest damn neighborhood in the city? Did she honestly think it didn't matter? A combination of anger and dismay shot through him and it was all he could do not to bang his head on the steering wheel. Just how rich were the Rileys, anyway? How was he going to fit in with this bunch, with his modest background and middle-class parents? Jason's lips tightened. The Rileys sure weren't going to find him worthy of their little girl—and they would be absolutely correct about that.

Damn—Emily had noticed his reaction and he could tell she didn't understand it. Maybe she thought he would be delighted to find out about her well-heeled background. Most men would have been, and the fact that he was not overjoyed and having a hard time hiding it was probably as confusing as hell to her. But he wasn't most men, and he wasn't at all thrilled she had kept something this important a secret.

* * *

What in the hell was wrong with Jason?

He looked at her childhood home with complete dismay. What was going through that head of his? Why did the sight of the admittedly grand house trigger a reaction like that? Sure, it implied wealth, something that would have delighted most men, and given his almost obsessive interest in the almighty dollar, it should have pleased him. But happy was not written all over his face, and that was damned confusing.

Another thing they needed to talk about. But not right now. Not when they were mere moments away from seeing her family. She forced a smile as she pointed to a spot along the wide, curving driveway several yards from the house. "Why don't you park over there?"

He appeared to shake off whatever was bothering him and pulled into the spot. They dragged their rolling suitcases across the driveway. She found her house key and opened the front door.

"Mom? Dad? Anybody here?"

"In the kitchen," her mother called. "You two come on back. You're the first ones to get here."

Emily took Jason's hand and half pulled him through the foyer, down the hall, then through the large, formally decorated living and dining room out to the big combination kitchen and family room that was the heart of the Riley home.

The delicious aroma of Patsy's baking permeated the air along with the flavorful notes of her wine-laced pot roast.

"This is where I got the idea to make that room flip on your house plans," Emily said as he stared at the floor-to-ceiling windows looking out onto the huge wrap-around patio and swimming pool.

"Yeah, but this one's a hell of a lot bigger," he murmured under his breath.

"So? The concept's the same."

She let go of his hand to join her mother in the kitchen. Patsy was putting a sheet of cookies into the oven and Alegra, her mother's longtime housekeeper, was peeling a pile of potatoes. Patsy engulfed Emily in a big hug and then turned to Jason, putting her arms around him.

"Welcome to our home, Jason," she said warmly, her smile friendly and encouraging.

Emily moved to Alegra and gave her a hug. "How are you, Alegra?"

"Bien, muy bien, Miss Emily." Alegra turned toward Jason. "Your boyfriend?"

"Yep, this is my boyfriend." She turned to Jason. "Jason, this is Alegra. She's practically a member of the family."

Jason smiled awkwardly. "Pleased to meet you, ma'am." He shook the hand Alegra offered.

"Was I-35 the usual nightmare?" Patsy asked.

"Worse," he said as he pointed to a plate of oatmeal-raisin cookies. "May I?"

Patsy nodded and Emily and Jason both picked up a cookie. "Damn, that's good," he enthused as he bit into the cookie. "Sugar free, I assume."

"Because of me, Mom's learned to make just about every dessert out there without sugar. Her recipes were featured in the last three Junior League cookbooks."

"That's awesome, Mrs. Riley," he said.

"Make it 'Patsy,' please. Now, let's go stash the suitcases."

Patsy led the way upstairs with Emily and Jason trailing behind her. "Emily's in her own room, of course. Jason, you're right here." She opened the door a little ways down from Emily's room. Emily's jaw nearly dropped. Boy, he was going to get a kick out of this. "And I put Holly and Jimmy and Carrie in the guest suite at the end of the hallway. Carrie can sleep on the sofa bed in the little sitting area. Russ is being Mister Independent. He's using the garage apartment."

Obediently, Jason put his suitcases in the indicated room while Emily stashed hers on her bed. Patsy headed downstairs, and Emily, her eyes dancing, opened the door to the bathroom she and Jason shared. She tiptoed through the bathroom and eased open the second door that led to the room Jason was using.

"Surprise," she said softly. "I underestimated Mom."

Jason whirled around and his mouth fell open. "What the—?" He peeked behind Emily to the common bathroom shared by both rooms and started to laugh. "So your mother's joined the twenty-first century after all. Good going, Mrs. Riley. I knew there was a reason I liked your mom."

* * *

Jason sat on the patio nibbling Patsy's cookies and looked around at the big, shady backyard; the same towering oak and pecan trees in front provided a lush canopy of shelter from the bright sun, except for the swimming pool and basketball court over to one side and a hot tub in one corner of the patio. Patsy had explained earlier that the expanded patio and outdoor kitchen were fairly recent additions and designed so that she and Mr. Riley could entertain the firm's clients in a casual setting.

Would Emily want an outdoor kitchen on her patio also? Jason made a mental note to ask her on the way back to College Station. If she wanted one, he'd put one in the plans immediately.

The patio door opened and he jumped up to help Emily with a huge pitcher of iced tea. "Daddy just got home and Russ pulled in right behind him. I expect Jimmy and Holly will be here in a few minutes. Mom thought it would be nice to have tea and cookies out here since the weather is so nice."

Jason set the pitcher on the big wrought-iron table. "Are you sure there isn't anything I can do to help?"

"According to Mom, you and everyone else with a Y chromosome can stay out of her way," she said wryly. "She says Holly and I are the only two she's trained well enough to help."

"I resent that statement," Russ Riley said as he stepped out on the patio bearing a foil-wrapped tray of cookies. "I know my way around the kitchen quite well, thank you very much." The cocky, good-looking soldier-turned-deputy sheriff put down the cookies and offered his hand to Jason. "How are you getting along these days?"

Russ turned to envelop Emily in a huge hug. "How are you doing, Em? Truthfully."

"My blood sugars haven't really settled down yet," she admitted. "Jason's ribs are still sore and his skin is still healing, even if he won't tell you that."

"I'm doing all right, Russ," Jason protested. "So are you and the other law-enforcement types through questioning that lunatic yet?"

"Yeah, for all the good it did. He's so out of it I doubt he'll ever even stand trial. If he does, it will be mainly your testimony and his fingerprints on the jimmy stick that will convict him."

"What about the other attacks?" Emily asked.

"Leigh Anne Navarro's murder is a slam-dunk, as is the grenade at Holly's house. Speaking of Holly, when are she and Jimmy and the munchkin showing up?"

"Any minute now," Ben Riley said as he stepped onto the patio with a stack of elegant outdoor china. He handed the plates to Russ and held out his arms to Emily. "How are you doing, baby?" he asked affectionately.

"Blood sugar's still bouncing around, but all right otherwise. Wade and Benny and I dunked our rings last night. Jason took us. "

Ben and Russ gasped. "Emily. What did that do to your blood sugar?" Ben demanded. He glared at both Emily and Jason.

"Not a thing, sir," Jason said smoothly, quickly hiding his poorly hidden resentment at the implication that he'd allow any harm to come to the woman he loved. "Emily dunked hers in unsweetened tea."

"Good grief, Daddy; Jason and I both have better sense than that," she scolded.

"I'm not sure about that." Russ shuddered. "Tea sounds worse than beer."

"Nonsense." Ben let go of his daughter and offered his hand to Jason. "And how are you feeling? Have you healed up yet?"

"My ribs are a bit sore and my skin's still tender." Jason hated making the admission, especially to Ben, but Emily had already told Russ the truth so it was pointless to prevaricate. "But I'm feeling a lot better."

"That's good." Ben sat down and motioned for Russ and Jason to join him.

"So how is your support group going, Jason?" Russ asked as he uncovered one of the plates and helped himself to a couple of cookies. "Holly told us at her last meeting that it had gotten pretty large."

Ben shot Russ a surprised look. "Didn't know you were going to Holly's meetings."

Russ shrugged. "I like hanging with them. I like being around other soldiers."

"Maybe if you hadn't been such a damned fool you could hang with a lot more of them," Ben grumbled.

Russ shot his father a go-to-hell look and opened his mouth to say something but Jason beat him to the punch. "I like being around other soldiers, too. And in answer to your question, Russ, it's gotten so big I had to move it to the meeting room in the basement at that little church down the street. A&M's crawling with wounded warriors trying to get their degrees or retrain for a job in the civilian market."

Russ came back with another question about Jason's group, and he was happy to talk with Russ about the support group while Ben listened quietly, his facial expression giving nothing away. But Jason wasn't a crackerjack salesman for nothing; he could read people like a book, and right now Ben Riley was far from sold on the idea of Jason as a husband to his baby girl.

That was going to change, Jason promised himself. He would win over Emily's old man if it was the last thing he did.

Ben stood up and offered to bring Russ and Jason a beer. They both declined and Ben and Emily wandered into the house. "So, not to change the subject, but have you offered your grandmother's ring to Emily yet?" Russ asked quietly.

Jason could feel his eyes widen. "How did you know I had Grandma's ring?"

"Your mom mentioned it the day Chucky attacked you. No, Mom and Dad don't know," Russ added when Jason glanced toward the house. "But Holly and Jimmy do." Russ picked up another cookie. "I'm not trying to pressure you or anything. I was just wondering."

Jason shook his head, not quite knowing how to take the question. "I have the ring but I haven't offered it to her yet. We still have a few things to work on before I do that."

"Gotcha. Just curious, that's all."

Was it Jason's imagination, or did Russ look just the tiniest bit relieved that Jason hadn't popped the question yet? He was being paranoid. Russ had been the epitome of friendly ever since the two had met the previous summer, and he owed Russ a lot for finally nailing the bastard who had almost taken his and Emily's lives.

But there was a world of difference in being warm and friendly to a fellow veteran, especially a wounded warrior, and picturing that same scarred man as a husband to his sister.

Jason could hear a bit of commotion inside the house before the patio door burst open and five-year-old Carrie Adamcik ran out onto the patio and straight into Russ's arms.

"Airborne!" she shouted as she hopped into Russ's lap. "I want to go airborne."

Russ laughed and stood with the little girl in his arms. Gently, he tossed Carrie into the air and caught her shrieking with delight as she fell back into his arms. "That was fun, Russ," she said. "Can you do it again?"

Jason watched as Russ tossed the little girl a second time. The patio door opened again and Emily and her sister Holly carried out thick poolside glassware and a stack of cloth napkins, the likes of which Jason had seen only in television commercials.

"Russ, don't let her give you a hernia," Holly said as she put down the glassware and ran a critical eye down both Emily and Jason. "You're both looking a whole lot better than the last time I saw you. I wish you could say the same about me." Holly did look a little paler than usual and had dark circles under her eyes.

"You look fine," Jason assured her quickly. He put his arms around her for a quick hug.

"Okay, Donahue, quit man-handling my woman," Jimmy Adamcik teased as he walked slowly and stiffly out on the patio. It had been almost a month since Jimmy had been hit by shrapnel and glass from Chucky's exploding grenade, and as the most seriously injured of the four of them, he still had a long way to go toward complete recovery. "But on the other hand, I'd like a hug from yours." Jimmy held open his arms and Emily gave him a careful hug.

After shaking hands with the men, Jimmy eased himself into one of the lounge chairs and motioned for Carrie to join him. Everyone made appreciative noises when Holly showed off her engagement ring. They had all poured themselves tea and were making short work of the cookies when Ben and Patsy finally joined them on the patio.

Ben made a beeline for Jimmy and shook his hand. "Good to have you here, son. How are you getting along these days?"

Son. Jason tried and failed to force down his resentment. He would win Ben over. He would show the old man he could be just as acceptable a husband as Jimmy Adamcik.

"I'm getting along slowly," Jimmy admitted. "Still not back at work. You know every day I miss in the office costs me money."

"It won't be much longer," Ben said encouragingly. "And Willis said he'd postponed all your courtroom work until you can get back there to do it. He told the complaining upstarts that you'd saved his niece from a grenade and he didn't give a damn if it took you a year to come back." Ben's brother was the county judge in front of whom Jimmy did most of his work.

"Besides, you can afford it," Holly piped up as she handed Carrie another cookie. "You got in the rest of the deer lease money in the mail this morning. You don't have to go back to work for months if you don't feel like it."

Deer lease money? On top of the fees Jimmy Adamcik made as an attorney? "I didn't realize you owned a ranch," Jason said.

"Yes, he owns the ranch just upstream from Jack Briscoe's place," Ben said. "It runs along the river as it turns into Lake Templeton."

Jimmy nodded. "Been in the family since the 1860s."

"Big old spread, if my memory serves me correctly," Russ said. "Several thousand acres. Dad and Uncle Willis took me hunting there a few times as a kid when Jimmy's father invited them."

"That was back in the days when my father used part of the ranch to raise cattle," Jimmy said. "When my father died some years back my mother sold all the cattle and we opened the entire ranch to hunting and started selling deer leases. It's been so successful we're going to add on to the old ranch house where the hunters stay. The only other thing I do with it is keep the horses up there." He glanced down at Carrie. "And I have my eye on maybe getting one more in the very near future. Next month, maybe."

"So what have you decided about running for Willis's bench?" Patsy asked. "Can you see yourself a county judge?"

"Yes, I'm definitely going to run. I think I can afford to pay for this campaign," Jimmy said as the rest of them laughed at a joke Jason didn't get.

Holy shit. Jimmy Adamcik was as loaded as the Rileys; not only did he make a boatload of money as an attorney, but deer leases in the Texas Hill Country didn't come cheap, and if Jimmy had several thousand acres to rent out he was probably making a killing. And he talked about buying Carrie a horse and paying for a political campaign as though they were nothing.

Jason could feel his already badly shaken self-confidence plummet. The job and the income he'd been so proud of back in College Station was beginning to look pretty paltry compared to what Jimmy Adamcik and Ben Riley brought to the table. Jason's newly acquired financial comfort couldn't hold a candle compared to what sounded like several generations of asset building in the Adamcik family. And how in the hell could Ben and Patsy Riley afford a damn mansion?

The conversation flowed around him as Jimmy and the Rileys talked about the upcoming campaign and mutual friends and relatives in Verde and Heaven's Point. The cookies and tea disappeared then Patsy and Emily wandered into the kitchen.

Holly said she needed their suitcases out of the car and Jimmy started to get up, but Jason leapt to his feet. "Stay put. I'll help Holly with the luggage."

Jimmy sank back down in the chair. "Thanks. Don't mind if you do."

At that moment a couple of college-aged boys tossed a basketball over the back fence and hopped into the Rileys' backyard. "Mr. Riley, you mind if we use your court to shoot a few hoops?"

Ben nodded and motioned them over. "Jimmy, Jason, our next-door neighbors Keller and Benson Dubose. Keller, Benson, Jason Donahue and Jimmy Adamcik. They're here with the girls."

The boys' eyes widened when they saw Jason up close but to their credit they did not stare. "Glad to meet you," the young men chorused. "Anybody want to join us?"

"Ya know…" Russ said thoughtfully, eyeing Jason up and down. "Want to challenge them to a pickup game?"

Jason grinned and nodded. "Let me get Holly's luggage and into a pair of shorts. Dudes, you're on."

Jason followed Holly out to Jimmy's Navigator. "You're limping more than usual," he observed as Holly unlocked the car. "Did something happen in Chucky's attack to aggravate the old injury?" She had been injured a couple of years back in an RPG attack and there had been no completely repairing her left leg.

"No. I've just been up on it too much since I've been taking care of Jimmy," she admitted as Jason started pulling out suitcases. "I must be up and down those stairs twenty-five times a day. I'm standing up in the kitchen to cook. And you wouldn't believe the laundry the three of us generate, which has to be carried upstairs to be put away. I'm getting a real taste of what being married to Jimmy's going to be like."

"And?" Jason prompted.

Holly's face broke into her trademark megawatt smile. "I'm loving every damned minute of it. So." She looked at Jason with a raised eyebrow. "Why am I the only Riley girl showing off her ring this weekend? Why isn't Emily showing hers off along with me?"

"Because I haven't given it to her yet?"

"Why not?"

"Do you want the politically correct answer I gave Russ or the truth?"

"Let's start with PC and then go for the truth."

"Okay. The politically correct version is that we are still working on a few things, which I suppose to some extent is the truth."

"Or is a pile of bullshit, depending on your point of view."

Jason laughed, "Yeah, there is that. Truth is. I'm scared shitless to ask her."

"For God sakes, why?" Holly looked stunned. "You know she loves you. Damn, she spent months trying to get your attention."

"Lots of reasons. A friggin' big one being the view in the mirror every morning. I'm ugly. Just plain ugly, and there's no getting around it. People don't see me with Emily. A case in point. Last night we were out together and this little bastard she has a class with tried to pick her up while she sat next to me holding my hand. Oh, and one of our neighbors was there last night and acted like she couldn't believe we were a couple."

"So what does any of that have to do with you and Emily? Why do you even give a damn what they think?"

"Because Emily sees the same ugly damn face they do. She says it doesn't matter, but how could it not? Plus, I'm a lot older than her. What if I pop the question? She'll look at me and decide she can do better."

"Glad to know thirty's over the hill, since I passed that landmark a few months ago," Holly said dryly. "I'll be sure to let Russ know, too. His is coming up next month."

"Damn it, that's not what I mean and you know it." Jason blew out an exasperated breath. "Look, a few months ago I was ugly, broke, and unemployed. Even now the only thing I have going for me is my income from my new job. I may not be in Jimmy Adamcik's league but I can at least give her a nice life. I just hope the money I'm making now is enough to offer your sister. I can't offer her much of anything else."

An odd expression crossed Holly's face. "Well, you'll never know if you don't ask her, now will you?" she asked quietly as she got out the rest of the suitcases and shut the back of the SUV. "Here, let's get these inside. I believe you have a date with a basketball."

* * *

Emily took the stairs two at a time with a pile of clean sheets and towels fresh from the dryer. Patsy and Alegra wouldn't need help with dinner, but with all the beds being made up and bathrooms stocked with linens, Alegra had gotten a bit behind with the laundry and, housekeeper or no, Emily was not above helping catch up on folding. She put the sheets in the linen closet and dutifully distributed the towels to the upstairs bathrooms and was back down the stairs when Jason and Holly came through the front door loaded down with multiple suitcases and duffel bags.

"Good grief, did you bring everything you own?" Emily laughed as she relieved Holly of a couple of the heavier-looking bags.

"I'm traveling with a five-year-old who wants to bring half her playroom," Holly said. "I knew Patsy and Daddy didn't have anything here for her to play with, so I let her bring a few things." She pointed to the guest suite at the end of the hall. "Patsy put us in there. Did she send Jason out to the garage apartment?"

"Nope, Russ is out there. She put Jason in Russ's old room," Emily giggled.

"*Really?*"

"I was surprised, too, but it sure works for me," Jason said, bringing up yet more heavy luggage.

"I think she doesn't want Daddy to know if and when Russ gets home tonight," Emily said thoughtfully. "Daddy's still royally pissed at Russ for getting the boot from Uncle Sam because of that woman."

"And Russ is behaving no better now that he's in Verde," Holly said. "He's running through women like a wino through Strawberry Hill." She looked at Jason. "Don't you have a date for a pickup basketball game?"

Jason disappeared into his assigned room and Holly looked at Emily and pointed into the guest suite. "I have a question for you." She tilted her head for Emily to follow her.

Damn. Holly was using her Captain Riley voice. Whatever her sister wanted to talk to her about, it wasn't going to be good.

Emily followed Holly into the two-room guest suite and shut the door behind her. "So what's got you snapping orders this afternoon?"

"You haven't told him about the damned trust fund yet, have you?" Holly demanded.

"No, I sure as hell haven't," Emily shot back. "And you know good and well why."

"Actually, I'm not sure I do," Holly said. "Yes, I get it that you tried the famous Alamo Heights millionaire alliance and had it fail, and then you had a bad experience with what's-his-face. But neither of those things really has anything to do with Jason, do they?"

"Yeah, they do, actually." Emily stopped and bit her lip. "Look, Holly, I don't know how to say this without making Jason look bad, but he has a shine for the dollar sign, big time. God knows I'm proud of him and how well he's doing at that new job, but really? Does he have to bring it up every time he turns around? Not only did he yammer about it to Mom and Daddy that night at dinner until I wanted to strangle him, but last night he actually brought it up to get rid of a guy that was hitting on me. Oh, it is *so* not funny," Emily hissed when Holly started laughing.

"Yes, it is," Holly sputtered. "Did it work?"

"Well, yeah, but Holly, it's what he said to me afterward that has me so worried. When I called him on it and said that somebody's bank account isn't the most important thing about them, he came out and said that sometimes it *is* the most important thing about somebody. Don't you get it? If I tell him now I'll never know if he loves me, plain diabetic little Emily Riley, or if it was the dollar signs that tipped the balance for him."

"He really said that?" Holly asked softly.

"He really did."

"Ouch," Holly said. "Put like that, I can see why you feel the way you do." Holly was quiet for a minute. "Have you ever thought that maybe Jason makes a big deal about the money because he's insecure about other things? Or that you're making a big deal about not telling Jason about your trust fund because you're insecure?"

"Him? Probably. And me? Definitely. And the sad thing is that we both probably have reason to be," Emily said quietly.

Holly shook her head and gave Emily a quick hug. "I'm still not sure you not telling him is the right thing to do, but I guess I understand why you want to wait. But please, don't wait too long. Secrets, even secrets kept for a reason, have a way of rising up and biting you right in the butt."

Emily nodded. "Yeah. I know." She didn't want to get into this any deeper with her sister; she barely wanted to think about it herself. "So. I understand there's about to be a basketball game. Want to go watch?"

Holly nodded and the two of them headed downstairs. The game was already in progress, Ben and Jimmy sitting in lawn chairs pulled up almost to the court. Holly and Emily flopped down on the ground, Emily curious as she watched Jason dribble the ball down the court and dunk it in the basket with considerable skill. She had never watched him play basketball before and hadn't realized how good he was at the game.

"Damn, I wish I could get out there and play with them," Jimmy groused.

"You won't be stove up forever. It won't be long before you're back at it," Holly reminded him.

"Was that your sport?" Emily asked.

"One of them. At a small-town high school you get to play them all. I was a clumsy but enthusiastic quarterback, a pretty decent center and a damn good pitcher."

"Thank God," Holly murmured. "Especially when it comes to pitching grenades."

Keller shot the ball toward the basket and Jason caught it in midair and passed it to Russ. Russ dribbled it down the court and tried to shoot, but the much taller Benson easily intercepted it and started toward his basket. Again, Jason caught the ball and started back down the court with it.

"Obviously, Jason has some experience under his belt," Holly observed when he easily shot the ball into the basket from halfway across the court. "Did he play in high school?"

"I think he said he played football in high school," Emily said.

"He played a lot of pickup basketball in Iraq," Jimmy said suddenly. "I used to go down and watch them play. He towered over most of the other soldiers and he was good, really good." Jimmy's mouth tightened. "That's where I noticed him first. Because of his size. I told his sergeant to put him on guard duty. I wanted the guards nice and big."

"No guilt trips, Major Adamcik," Holly said crisply. "Things happen when you're fighting a war."

"It wasn't your fault he and the others got hurt that day," Ben added.

"That's right," Emily chimed in. "Jason certainly doesn't hold you responsible."

"Good to know," Jimmy murmured, head down.

Keller caught the ball and started toward the basket. Jason and Russ started after him but Jason stopped suddenly, stumbling a little, and bent over with his hands on his knees, gasping as he rocked back and forth unsteadily. Russ and Emily both raced toward him, Russ grabbing him on one side and Emily the other when he would have tumbled to the concrete. They let him wheeze for a minute before turning him around and half dragging him off the court and pushing him into the lawn chair Ben had vacated.

"Jason, are you all right?" Emily demanded as he propped his head in his hands and continued to gasp and wheeze. She turned frightened eyes onto Holly and Russ. "I've never seen this happen to him before."

"Okay. I-I'm okay," Jason gasped. "Just-just winded."

Keller and Benson approached Jason cautiously. "Man, if it's something we did, we're sorry."

"Not. You-your doing," Jason wheezed. "B-bad lungs."

"Did you get too hot?" Emily asked. She put her hand on Jason's back. "You are overheated. Can somebody get him a glass of cold water and a wet towel?"

"On it." Russ took off for the house at a trot.

"Emily—I—-

"Just sit a minute, Jason," Emily said soothingly. "You need to get your breath back. Russ is bringing water and a towel."

Russ returned a moment later with a bottle of water and a dripping bath towel, which Emily draped over Jason's shoulders. He sat quietly as the gasping stopped and his breathing returned to normal then motioned for the bottle of water.

"Are you going to be all right now?" Holly asked.

Jason nodded then grinned crookedly at the Dubose boys. "Sorry to spoil a good basketball game."

"Aw, that's nothing. We're just glad you're all right." They picked up the basketball. "See everybody tomorrow." The boys wandered off to a chorus of 'Bye' and 'See you later.'

"What happened, Jason?" Ben asked quietly. "One minute you were fine and the next you could barely breathe."

Emily felt Jason stiffen beside her. "Probably a combination of things, Mr. Riley. Because of the damage to my lungs from the explosion that burned me, I get winded easily. My ribs are still sore from Chucky's tire iron. And because of the scarring I get overheated. No big deal, honestly."

Ben looked at Jason thoughtfully. "You know, because of Holly I know a little about wounded warriors and their injuries, but I've always thought more in terms of the kinds of aftereffects she's had to deal with. I never really thought about burns and how they can affect someone long-term. Just how badly have the burns affected your overall health?"

Jason's head snapped up and he looked Ben in the eye. "I may look like hell and not be worth shit on a basketball court, sir, but I'm perfectly capable of standing on a showroom floor for twelve hours at a stretch to make a living."

Ben's eyes narrowed as Holly and Jimmy shot one another a glance. *Where in the hell had that come from?*

"Jason does fine, Daddy, honestly," Emily said quickly. "Considering what he's been through he's really a very healthy man."

"It's like it is with me, Daddy," Holly added. "There are aftereffects but we cope. Right, Jason?"

Jason nodded. "That's right, Mr. Riley. There are aftereffects but we learn to cope. And most of the time we do just fine."

Chapter Five

Emily held Jason's hand as they strolled down San Antonio's Riverwalk, that famous stretch of the San Antonio River that meandered through the heart of the beautiful old city. Located a story below street level, the Riverwalk was lined with shops, restaurants, bars, and hotel lobbies and thronged with tourists and locals alike.

Music spilled out of the open doors of the pubs and bars while mariachi bands wandered around the tables at the open-air restaurants serenading diners. Long, flat-bottomed barges chugged up and down the river carrying sightseers and the occasional dinner party amidst the aroma of steaks, enchiladas, and smoky barbeque ribs floating through the cool November air.

Jason pointed to a little girl holding her mother's hand as her indulgent father bought her a lighted tiara from a sidewalk vendor. The child shrieked with delight as her mother carefully placed the tiara on her head. "There, now you're Daddy's princess," the mom told the little girl while her father beamed.

"What a pretty little girl," Emily said as the young family disappeared into the crowd. "I wish Jimmy and Holly had been able to bring Carrie down here tonight."

"Maybe they can the next time they come down," Jason said. "Besides, tonight I'd rather have you to myself." He leaned down and gave Emily a tender kiss on her cheek. "It's so pretty here. Just the place to romance my sweetie."

And to get away from the Riley clan for a few hours. Although Ben had said nothing, Emily knew her father well; he had not appreciated Jason's reaction to what she hoped was honest curiosity, not implied criticism of Jason as a potential partner. And she knew Jason well. Clearly, he had taken offense to Ben's question.

Even though he was perfectly gracious to everyone at dinner, Jason was not his usual relaxed, charming, funny self. Maintaining a warm, friendly façade in front of the Riley family had been work. When she suggested a visit downtown, he jumped at the opportunity.

This disconnect between Jason and her father had to be temporary. Ben would have to warm to Jason as his son-in-law. Bumps aside, yeah, she was all in; Jason was it for her.

"If you think it's pretty tonight, just wait until Friday when they turn on all the Christmas lights," she commented. "Every tree for the entire two–and-a-half-mile stretch will be lit up. We always come down here to see them sometime during the week before Christmas. Mom says she can't put the turkey in the oven until she's seen the lights."

"Your mom does all the holidays for the family?" Jason asked. "My mom and my aunt switch off."

"She does now that Grandma Harrington's gotten too old and Uncle Shell got a divorce."

"I'm sure she does a great job if that dinner she and Alegra put on the table tonight was anything to go by. That roast of hers was out of this world. She wouldn't have happened to teach you to make it like that, would she?" He grinned.

"Actually, she taught me and Holly, who said Jimmy and Carrie both love it. And yeah, I'll make you some soon." She pointed up toward a curio shop that was on the street level. "I used to love the junk they sell in there. Let's go take a peek."

Jason followed her up the winding metal staircase and into the little shop, bursting with all things Texas kitschy. "What? No serapes?" he teased when Emily tried on a fringed leather jacket.

"Actually, if you want to see the true Mexican imports I need to take you to El Mercado. They sell the Talavera pottery and the guayabera shirts there."

"Maybe next time. Do you want the jacket?"

"Nah." As she put it back on the rack, she caught Jason's frown. "I have enough jackets already," she explained.

They ducked into a few more shops, emerging empty-handed from each of them. When the smoky riff of a bluesy saxophone drifted out into the evening air, he pointed toward the source of the seductive melody. "Let's go listen awhile."

After he paid their cover, the hostess settled them at a small table in the back. The band wove their magic; the plaintive duet of the saxophone and equally haunting clarinet created a melody and harmony that was almost magical. She glanced over at Jason and could tell he too was under the spell of the mesmerizing tune.

The next few numbers were like that, slow and seductive, and Jason pulled Emily's chair closer to his and slipped his arm over the back. "What time does the Riley clan go to bed?" he whispered in her ear.

"Not for a couple of hours, and I'll be damned if I'm going upstairs first. We'll have to be patient."

Jason laughed and nibbled her ear. As the band excused themselves for a much-needed break, she was about to suggest they leave when she spotted a couple paying their cover at the door and felt herself go cold inside. Of all the bars and clubs in downtown San Antonio, why did Brandon Bentley and his latest Barbie *du jour* have to show up here?

Maybe Brandon wouldn't notice her, she hoped silently as she turned her head slightly away from the door. But no such luck; out of the corner of her eye she saw Brandon point her out to his date. She steeled herself as he steered his date across the floor to where she and Jason were sitting.

"Well, hello, Emily," he said, his movie-star handsome face smiling and his voice as smooth as the expensive whiskey he loved. "It's been awhile."

"Hasn't it, though," she said dryly, smashing down the urge to slap Brandon across his too-pretty face, instead calling forth the gracious southern belle persona Patsy had drilled into her for occasions such as this.

"Brandon, this is my boyfriend, Jason Donahue." She turned to Jason, ignoring the shock on Brandon's face when Jason turned his scarred features in Brandon's direction. "Jason, this is Brandon Bentley." She turned to Brandon's drop-dead beautiful date. "And you would be?"

The girl flashed a smile that froze when she turned to Jason. "I'm Chrissie," she murmured as she quickly averted her eyes from Jason. "So glad to meet you."

"Likewise," Jason said smoothly as he shook Brandon's hand. He looked from Brandon to Emily. "Old friends from the neighborhood?"

"Not exactly," Emily said tightly.

"Nope, Emily and I were an item for a while," Brandon said. "I almost persuaded her to marry me. Wish I'd succeeded."

"Oh, really?" Jason said. "Emily's never mentioned you."

Brandon gave a careless shrug. "I suppose she has her reasons. So how have you been?"

Like you really give a damn. "I've been great." She nailed Brandon with a pointed stare. "And you?"

Brandon smiled faintly. "Okay, I guess. Once I got over losing you. I'll admit it was hard at first, though."

"Oh, sweetie, I'm sure you weren't lonely for too long," Emily purred as she glanced at Chrissie. She stood up, practically pulling Jason to his feet. "Since Jason and I were about to call it a night, why don't you take this table? I don't see too many vacant ones at the moment."

"I have a better idea. Why don't you two sit back down and I'll buy us a round of drinks?" Brandon said smoothly. "We can all get to know one another better."

For a second Emily was tempted. It would've been fun to turn Jason loose on the lazy, unemployed Brandon. But if the topic of money came up, inevitably so would her trust fund, and that was not happening, especially coming from Brandon.

She shot Jason a *No way, José* look, which he acknowledged with a slight nod and the two of them wished Brandon and Chrissie a good evening.

Maneuvering the crowded sidewalk of the Riverwalk in silence, the romantic mood of the evening had shattered beyond recovery. He wants to know, she thought as Jason glanced occasionally in her direction. He'll ask who Brandon had been to her and why she reacted to the bastard the way she did.

But what could she tell Jason and not give away the existence of the trust fund? Was now the time to tell him about the money? Or should she stick to her original plan and wait?

She would wait, although now it felt more like deception than a lie of omission.

* * *

Damn, that guy was a looker, Jason thought bitterly as he glanced down at Emily's pensive expression. He had never been that good looking in his life. Ever. Was she lying to him when she said his scars didn't matter? And why had she not once, in all the months they had been together, ever even mentioned the son of a bitch that clearly upset her?

She took a deep breath before blurting out. "I caught him in bed with another woman. A really beautiful woman."

Well, that explained a lot. "Had he already asked you to marry him?"

"He was at the dropping-hints-like-crazy stage." Kind of like he and Emily were now, Jason reflected. "He'd given me a key to his place and I went over to surprise him with a home-cooked dinner. And there they were."

"What did he say to you?"

Emily paused a minute and Jason could tell she was thinking about her answer. "You know, it really doesn't matter exactly what he said to me that afternoon. The fact that he was screwing a drop-dead gorgeous woman and didn't understand why I had a problem with that pretty much told me all I needed to know."

That seemed like half a story. "There has to be more to it than that."

Emily shot him a go-to-hell look. "I don't know why there would be. I fell for him, I learned I couldn't trust him, I dumped his sorry ass. End of story. Lesson learned."

"And what lesson was that?"

"Not to be so naïve and gullible when it comes to men," she said tersely. "Look. Brandon Bentley was an embarrassing and painful episode in my past, and frankly, I would prefer that it stay in my past. Can you let me do that, please?"

"Sure, honey. I'm sorry he hurt you," he said softly while his sixth sense picked up all kind of vibes that said she was hiding something. The question was—what?

They drove home in silence, both lost in their own thoughts. The household had mostly gone to bed, but Patsy was curled up on the sofa reading; she gave them a wave before going back to her story.

"Want to raid the fridge?" Emily asked.

"I could eat again."

They shared a plate of cheese and crackers at the breakfast bar before climbing the stairs. "Do you want me to join you for a little while?" he whispered as she opened her bedroom door.

"Sure. But we'll have to be quiet," she said against his lips.

He went into his room long enough to strip out of everything but his T-shirt and boxers. Emily was waiting for him in the small twin bed of her girlhood wearing a Mickey Mouse T-shirt and an unreadable expression on her face.

Deciding not to pursue what would surely be a heated topic, he gave over to his baser nature. "What, no sexy teddy?" he teased as he stripped off his remaining clothes and pulled the T-shirt over her head.

"Maybe tomorrow night," she patted the bed beside her. "Let's see if we can both fit on this little bitty ol' bed of mine."

"I think we can manage" Trying to slide beside her, he reconsidered. "On second thought, this is smaller than that pile of lumps in College Station. There's barely room for us both to lie down."

"Only one of us needs to be lying on the bed," she said as he framed her face with his hands and captured her lips in a searing kiss that scorched him to his soul. "Make love to me, Jason. I need you so much."

Bodies entwined on the narrow bed, they made love with heat and passion and a hint of desperation. Hand and mouths and bodies came together as he sought to imprint his claim on the woman he loved.

He would fucking well make her forget Brandon damn Bentley, Jason thought as he trailed a line of hot wet kisses down her stomach and yet further, pushing her legs apart roughly so he could dive into the core of her pleasure.

By the time he was done, the thought of the other man would never cross her mind he promised as he sucked and caressed, forcing her to come apart for him over and over.

Mine.

He rose above her trembling body, pushing in before she had come down from her last climax, claiming her; their bodies melded together so completely he left no doubt they were made to be together. Over and over he thrust, ensuring she would fly as she'd never soared before, vowing they would be joined together forever.

Totally spent, their faces buried in each other's neck, she nuzzled while murmuring. "Incredible."

That should have been enough. He should've reveled in the musky scent of their sex and held her close. But his mouth moved before his brain kicked in. "Do you still love him? Does he still matter to you?"

"Oh, *hell* no," Emily said bitterly, kicking out her legs and pushing against his chest, effectively rolling him onto the floor. Pulling her T-shirt over her head, she bit out. "I may have loved him once, but those days are over and done with."

Venom glared at him as he shoved his legs into his boxers then grabbed up his shirt. Yeah, it might've been an asshole time to bring up the perfect-looking Brandon Bentley, but her reaction to him was more than she admitted. If she didn't still care about the bastard, then why had she worn that pinched, hurt expression on their walk to the car and the whole way back to her folks' house?

Crossing through the adjoining bathroom, Jason recalled Brandon's almost pretty face and stopped short as a thought crossed his mind—what if she was with him on the rebound? What if she was interested in him *because* he was unattractive? After all, she had chased him. What if her interest had been calculated? She had been so badly hurt by a handsome man that she was determined not to go back there? Right. Why not hook up with an ugly guy the next time? Why not find the ugliest, homeliest SOB out there and get involved with him? Maybe the ugly guy would at least be faithful.

And now, was she getting tired of looking at him and wanted her good-looking lover back? Did she still love the bastard, even after he'd cheated on her? Jason tried to tell himself not to be ridiculous, that Emily wasn't that kind of person. He tried to tell himself that suspecting such a thing was unworthy of him and unfair to her, but the idea had taken hold and put down roots.

Jason was damned if he knew how to get rid of it.

* * *

Jason surfaced from a fitful slumber to the sound of terrified screaming in the night. Holy shit, another poor bastard's having the nightmare from hell, he thought tiredly as he debated whether to get out of bed himself or let one of the other patients or a night nurse wake the man. When he turned over, determined to let someone else take care of the problem tonight, his eyes snapped open; he realized he wasn't in the hospital or in College Station at his apartment, but in a spare bedroom in Ben and Patsy Riley's house in San Antonio—and the terrified screaming was coming from the guest suite at the end of the hall.

God in heaven, that was Jimmy screaming, probably in the middle of a flashback. Everyone knew Jimmy had PTSD, but knowing it was one thing; listening to the man's screams of terror were quite another.

Not bothering with a robe, Jason ran down the hall and pushed into the guest suite, cringing as Jimmy's piercing screams tore through the air, even louder now that there were no walls to muffle them.

Jason snapped on the light to the sitting room and found Carrie curled up on the sofa bed clutching a stuffed bear, her little eyes wide with terror.

"Daddy's dreaming and Holly needs help," she said. "Can you help her?"

"You bet I can, sweetheart," Jason said. He whirled around as Emily burst through the sitting room door, Ben and Patsy on her heels. "Jimmy's having a flashback," Jason told the three of them. "Emily, Patsy, you get Carrie downstairs. Holly's going to need my help."

Emily and Patsy nodded. "Come on, Carrie," Emily said as she took the little girl by the hand. "Jason and Holly will help your daddy. I bet we can find a few more of Mom's cookies down there."

"I saved some just for you," Patsy said. They all cringed as Jimmy let loose with another particularly blood-curdling yell.

"Go help Holly," Carrie pleaded. "The last time Daddy had a dream like this he hurt her."

Jason turned his attention to the darkened bedroom where Jimmy was thrashing around on the bed and Holly was unsuccessfully trying to wake him.

"No, don't turn on the light," Jason said sharply as Ben reached toward the light switch. "That will just make it worse." He leaned down over the terrified man caught in his personal nightmare. "Okay, let's see if we can get him out of this."

Jimmy sat up, nearly bumping heads with Jason. "No, no, get back. It's a trap. Damn it, *get back.*" He screamed at the horror only he could see.

"Jimmy, wake up," Holly beseeched. She reached out her hand and Jimmy pushed it away roughly. "Damn it, I can usually bring him out of these before he's in this deep, but this one's a doozy."

"You better move before he hurts you. Let me get beside him. I can restrain him if I have to." Jason motioned Holly away and took her place on the bed. "Jimmy, wake up."

"No! Get away from me, get back, it's a fucking trap," Jimmy yelled. "The baby's wired. Get the hell back!"

"Oh, shit," Jason said as he met Holly's eyes. "He's dreaming about the baby suicide bomber, isn't he? He's dreaming about me and the others. He's dreaming about the day I got blown up."

Holly nodded. "He dreams about you a lot."

"Well, *hell.*" Jason turned Jimmy around, holding his flailing arms securely when he tried to push him away. "Major Adamcik, calm down, it's going to be all right. We're not there anymore, Major Adamcik. We're here. We're home. We're safe. Nobody's going to get hurt tonight. It's all right."

Maybe it was the deep timbre of Jason's voice, or maybe it was command in his words, but Jimmy stopped thrashing and his eyes snapped open.

"What? Where?" He looked around the darkened room at Jason and Holly, then at Ben Riley standing stock-still in the corner. "God *damn* it," Jimmy ground out as he buried his head in his shaking hands. "Son of a goddamn bitch. I thought I was getting better." He glanced toward the door to the sitting room. "Did I wake Carrie up, too? Is she all right?"

"She's fine. She's downstairs with Patsy and Emily," Holly said softly. She reached out and grasped Jimmy's hands in her own. "It's all right, Jimmy. Dr. Jacobsen said we could expect these now and again, especially after the episode with Chucky."

"But I wasn't dreaming about Chucky. I was dreaming about..." Jimmy looked at Jason with horror on his face.

Jason nodded. "I know. You were dreaming about the day I got slammed." Jimmy winced. "I remember it. You saw something and yelled at us to get back. We tried, but…" Jason stood up. "Holly, where can I find Jimmy a fresh T-shirt? This one's soaked. And where's his meds?"

"Shirt's in the black suitcase and his meds are in the dopp kit in the bathroom. Two pills and a little water to wash them down." Holly didn't let go of Jimmy's hands.

Jason found a T-shirt and tossed it on the foot of the bed. Ben followed Jason into the bathroom and wet a washrag. "Do we need to call a doctor?" Ben whispered.

"I don't think so," Jason said as he unearthed Jimmy's prescription and shook out the two pills. "If he's awake and aware there's really nothing to be done but to give him a little time to come down off the cliff. Mostly he just needs a chance to chill."

Ben glanced into the bedroom then shut the bathroom door. "Carrie said something about Jimmy hurting Holly during a flashback. Is Jimmy a danger to my daughter?"

Jason took a deep breath and chose his words carefully. "The story I heard is that he was in the middle of a flashback and trying to push her away to safety and knocked her into a doorjamb. Holly knows now that if he gets like that again she needs to get somebody to help her."

He turned to face Ben. "Sir, I know you have your doubts about me being the man you want for Emily, and maybe those doubts are justified. But I beg you, please, *please* don't hold the PTSD against Jimmy. He's a good, gentle country lawyer who went to war, saw things no one should ever have to see, and came home just as badly wounded as Holly and I did. The only difference is that his wounds don't show." Ben scanned Jason's face. "Insult to injury, he and Holly were almost killed by that madman, and now he's got another trauma to work through along with visible scars to accompany the invisible ones. He can't help the PTSD any more than I can help this ugly damn face or Holly can help the migraines and the limp."

"Do you get them, too? The nightmares?"

"A few. Not like he does."

"I see." Ben handed the damp washrag to Jason. "If you think it would help him relax I can take the cover off the hot tub. The water's already warm."

"Why don't you ask him? That might be just the thing."

"Thank you for helping him tonight. How did you know what to do?"

"I was in the hospital for three years, Mr. Riley. I got very good at helping the newbies. And I've answered a few emergency calls from the members of my support group or their significant others on occasions such as tonight."

"It's good of you to help them," Ben said.

Jason shrugged. "They would do the same for me."

Jimmy agreed to the hot tub and Ben went down to get it ready. Jason gave Jimmy his pills while he wiped his face and Holly unearthed a pair of board shorts. Unmindful of his nudity, Jimmy stripped off his boxers and put on the shorts. Fresh shrapnel scars peppered his back, butt and the back of his legs, red and angry-looking.

"Hurt like a son of a bitch, I'll bet," Jason said matter-of-factly as Jimmy pulled on the fresh T-shirt.

"Better my ass than Holly's face. Speaking of." He leaned down and gave Holly a tender kiss. "Go on back to bed. I'll be all right."

"Are you sure?" she asked anxiously.

"I'll go down with him," Jason volunteered. He held up his hand when Jimmy started to object. "I could use a little chill therapy myself."

Jason unearthed a couple of towels from the bathroom then trooped downstairs with Jimmy. Patsy and Emily were sitting with Carrie at the breakfast bar, an empty plate and cup in front of her.

"Daddy, are you all right?" the little girl asked as she jumped off the stool and ran to her father.

Jimmy knelt down beside his daughter. "Daddy's fine," he said as he hugged the child. "He's even going out to the hot tub for a little while. Did you have some more of Patsy's good cookies?"

"I did, and she said I could call her Grandma Patsy if I wanted to."

"And I bet you do, don't you?" She nodded. "How about you go on back up to bed? Holly's upstairs waiting for you." Jimmy looked up and mouthed 'Thank you' to Patsy and Emily.

"Come on, Carrie," Emily said as she took Carrie's hand. "Off to bed." She turned hooded eyes in Jason's direction. "See you in the morning."

Jason and Jimmy walked out to the hot tub, its steaming water frothing from the multiple jets. They pulled off their shirts and eased into the foaming water. "Are you going to get overheated?" Jimmy asked as Jason eased his scarred legs and chest down into the water.

"Nah, it's not that hot, and I'm not moving around," Jason answered.

Jimmy got a pack of cigarettes and a lighter out of his pocket before lowering himself down into the tub. He put a cigarette to his lips with trembling fingers. "This is the only time I let myself indulge in this filthy habit. After a flashback."

"Beats drinking." Jason smiled.

The men sat, the whir of the water the only sound while Jimmy smoked his cigarette.

"I hate it when I have the damn things," he said suddenly. "They embarrass the hell out of me." He stubbed out his cigarette in the tub-side ashtray. "And now Holly's dad's going to be looking at me and wondering if he wants his little girl hooking up with the local bat-shit crazy lawyer. Christ, he probably thinks I shouldn't run for judge."

"Join the club. He's not too fond of the local shish kebab either." Jimmy winced and Jason laughed out loud. "Hey, man, we gotta laugh sometimes about it all or we're just gonna cry. And I've shed my share of tears and I bet you have, too."

"A few," Jimmy admitted. "That day you were hurt and the others were killed. I went back to my tent and cried like a damn baby."

"I cried the day they handed me a mirror and let me see the new and improved Jason Donahue. Threw the damn mirror across the room and broke it and cried for three days straight, until my sharp-tongued mother came to see me and asked me if I really wanted to trade places with my dead buddies. Put a stop to that pity party real quick. Not that I haven't had a few others." He turned to Jimmy. "But then there are the times, like tonight, when I hear you having the flashback from hell, or the night of the Verde Homecoming, when I watched Tommy Joe wheel his chair into the place or when Cathy and Beto danced on their prostheses, that I think, maybe I didn't get such a raw deal after all. Unlike my buddies, I do still have a life."

"Even if it's not the life you thought you were going to have," Jimmy mused.

Jason shrugged. "It's close enough." He stared up at the lights of an airplane in the sky. "I wish you didn't dream about that day. There wasn't a thing you could have done differently that would have changed things."

"So says you and the rest of the universe. Try convincing my subconscious of that little fact."

"Does being around me trigger your nightmares? Is being around me in the future going to be a problem for you?"

"The first time I saw you that day at the picnic it did." Jimmy's honesty made Jason cringe inside. "But since then, no. Don't blame yourself for this one. I've had more than one since my little encounter with Chucky, just not this bad." He looked at Jason and grinned. "Why? Are you planning to be around me a lot in the future?"

Jason looked at Jimmy pensively. "I sure hope so. But I don't know. We ran into one of Emily's old boyfriends earlier and she didn't say two words for the rest of the way home. I'm afraid she's still pining for the handsome son of a bitch. Handsome being the operative word here."

"Or she might have been thinking about what a jerk the guy was and how badly he hurt her," Jimmy said. "Jason, don't start borrowing trouble. Your looks aren't a problem. Emily saw past your scars from the first, didn't she? Besides, you're doing well at your new job and you've treated her like a princess. What more could Emily ask than that?"

"I hope you're right," Jason said slowly. Perhaps Jimmy knew what he was talking about, but Jason couldn't unknot his doubts.

Chapter Six

Emily perched on the stool at Patsy's breakfast bar and watched her mother mix up a batch of homemade cornbread. "How many of those do you have to cook up for the dressing?" she asked as Patsy poured the batter into a greased cast iron skillet.

"Today I'm making three," she said as she popped the cornbread into the heated oven. "Alegra made the biscuits two days ago and put them through the Cuisinart yesterday, but somehow with everybody coming we didn't get as far as the cornbread." Patsy put a pod in the coffeemaker and flipped the handle.

"I was tempted to tell your father to just take us all out to eat but I hate to do that to your grandmother. This is her mother's turkey dressing and Mom's gotten too frail to cook it herself anymore."

"Besides, how could Granddad have his usual field day ragging on all us grandkids in front of everybody in a restaurant?" Emily teased. "Gotta have the privacy of your daughter's home to do that."

Patsy rolled her eyes. "I swear, he's gotten almost obsessed with this business of wanting all of you to go to law school and join the firm. That's all he can talk about—why you three haven't shown any interest in joining the firm like Kevin and his wife did. He's especially incensed that Russ is working as a small-town deputy, now that he's out of the Army. He thinks Russ really should be an attorney."

"I thought he'd be more upset that Russ got himself booted out of the Army."

"Nope, your father's the one angry with him about that. Well, well, speak of the devil," Patsy drawled as Russ wandered in the patio doors, bright-eyed but unshaven. "What time did you finally drag yourself home?"

"Yeah, what time did you get in? It must have been late since you missed all the excitement," Emily added.

"What excitement?" Russ asked as he moved his mother's coffee off the machine and put in a pod for his own cup.

"Jimmy had the flashback from hell and Jason stepped in and took care of everything," Patsy said. "Rather masterfully, too. I was very impressed with that young man last night."

"Good for Jason. Can't say I'm surprised, though. It's common practice in the military hospitals for the patients to help out some," Russ said. "And I imagine he's helped his support group also. So how bad was it last night?"

"Bad," Patsy and Emily said in unison.

"I've never heard screaming like that," Patsy admitted. "Does Jimmy have an especially bad case of PTSD?"

"He doesn't have an especially good case," Russ said dryly. "So where is everybody?"

"Daddy's in his office catching up on paperwork, Jimmy's still asleep, I'm on cooking duty with Mom, and Jason volunteered to take Holly and Carrie to the zoo. Holly wanted Jimmy to have a chance to rest before dinner tonight and Carrie was wired."

"Nice of Jason to take them," Russ observed. "Since Alegra's with her family, Mom, my Y-chromosome notwithstanding, I'd be happy to help you and Emily with the cooking."

"Works for me," Patsy said brightly. "You two can start by getting all those vegetables out of the back refrigerator and peeling and slicing them for the vegetable tray."

Russ returned with bags of veggies then he and Emily got to work. "So how did Jason like being the hero last night?" Russ teased. "Does he think he made any headway with Dad?"

Emily shrugged. "He didn't say."

In truth, she and Jason hadn't said much of anything to one another this morning. She was still angry with him for bringing Brandon up the way he did, but the anger was fading and an uneasiness at the chasm between them was taking its place.

Jason had been quiet and uncommunicative, which, given the loaded questions he'd lobbed at the absolute wrong time—*"Do you still love him? Does he still matter to you?"*—didn't surprise her at all. The tension between them hung in the air like the stench of manure in a feedlot.

Of course she didn't love Brandon Bentley anymore, but if she told Jason why she'd have to tell him the entire story, including the existence of the trust fund. But she was going to have to do that sooner or later anyway. Jason knew he hadn't gotten the whole story and he deserved more consideration from her than that. She owed Jason the truth, and it was time she owned up to that and leveled with him about the money, even though the thought terrified her down to her bones.

What if…no, she wasn't going to go there. She would tell him before the weekend was out, proposal or not. She'd go ahead and tell him the whole truth about Brandon, and she would tell him about the trust fund. Fingers crossed, he wouldn't be impressed and it wouldn't make a difference. She needed him to love her for herself, plain little diabetic Emily Riley. No falling dazzled and thrilled at the feet of the Riley family heiress.

* * *

Jason stood patiently outside the ladies' room where Holly had disappeared with Carrie moments before. A cool front had blown in, sweeping away the hazy early morning clouds and turning the sky a crisp, eye-popping blue.

He leaned against the wall and watched the parade of giggling teenagers, hand-holding couples, parents and grandparents trying to keep up with small children, and the occasional extended family taking advantage of the zoo's doors-open three-hundred-sixty-five days a year policy.

An elderly man sporting a Vietnam veteran ball cap caught Jason's eye, nodded, and smiled. "Wounded warrior?" he asked.

"Yes, sir, I am," Jason said. "You serve, too?"

"Three tours," the old man said proudly. "Thank you for your service, son."

"And thank you for yours."

The old man tipped his hat and walked away. Holly and Carrie ducked out of the restroom, Carrie clutching Holly's hand and trying to pull ahead of the limping Holly. "Here, munchkin, take my hand instead," Jason said. "Holly's tired and her leg hurts."

"You can say that two or three more times," Holly said as she gratefully relinquished the energetic child to Jason. "I didn't get back to sleep until almost morning."

"I'm sorry if I kept Jimmy downstairs too long," Jason said. "I thought he needed to talk."

In fact, he and Jimmy had spent the better part of two hours in the hot tub, talking or not as the spirit led them. Jason told Jimmy about growing up in Austin, his years in the A&M Corps of Cadets and his decision to enlist. Jimmy talked about growing up in Verde and his life as a young husband with Carrie's mother Lauren, and the nightmare of losing her to cancer. Although no more was said about Emily, Jimmy was very encouraging when Jason talked about his success at his new job and the house he wanted to build. Jimmy Adamcik seemed to be a genuinely decent person, and Jason came away with an even higher opinion of his former major than before.

"He did need to talk," Holly said. "And I'm so grateful you were here for him to talk with."

"Oh, it was mutual," Jason said. "We talked a little about my situation as well as his."

Carrie pointed in the direction of the huge netted aviary. "Can we go in there?" she asked excitedly. "I love birds."

"Sure, munchkin," Jason said. They trooped over to the aviary and Jason helped get Holly and Carrie through the double-door system and into the lushly green enclosure lined with wooden walkways and teeming with bright, chirping birds.

"So what situation of yours did you talk about?" Holly asked. "Are you still angsting over whether to propose to Emily?"

"Do bears shit in the woods? Yes, I'm still *angsting*, as you put it." He let go of Carrie's hand so she could get a little closer to a brightly colored parrot. "I'm beginning to think she wouldn't be happy with me, not long-term." He shoved his hands in his pockets.

"And you think this because?" Holly asked.

"We ran into her old boyfriend last night," Jason said tersely. "The one she almost married that she hadn't bothered to tell me about."

"Which one was that? The nice one or the asshole?" Holly said.

"What do you mean, which one? There were *two*?"

"Oops," Holly murmured.

"The asshole, I guess," Jason muttered. "The really good-looking one. The one who cheated on her. She grabbed me and got us out of there so fast it would make your head swim, and then she didn't have two words to say for the rest of the evening. She's been off in her own little world ever since we ran into the bastard. Damn it, Holly, she still cares about the motherfucker."

"I don't think that's necessarily the case," Holly said evenly. "Did you ask her how she felt?"

"Of course I asked her and of course she said no. But if she doesn't love him, then why did she react so strongly when she saw him? Why does he still matter that much to her?"

Holly sighed. "I'm not sure, Jason. You're going to have to get her to tell you that." Holly's sidestepping was not good juju.

"God damn it, at this point, how do I get her to tell me anything?"

"For crying out loud, Jason, man up and propose to her. What's the worst thing that can happen?"

"She says no. Or she says yes even though she cares about somebody else and would down deep rather be with him," Jason said stubbornly.

"Or she says yes because she loves you and you get to live happily ever after." Holly threw up her hands in frustration. "Damn it, Jason. Quit worrying about the other guy and ask."

"It's not that easy." He hated saying this again, but couldn't think of another way to put his feelings into words. "I'm scared."

"BFD, you're scared. So was every man that ever proposed to a woman. Grow a pair and get on with it."

"A pair of what?" Carrie, who had wandered back to them asked, puzzled.

Holly looked down at Carrie and groaned. "Nothing, sweetie."

Jason had to bite his lip to keep from laughing. He stood at attention and popped Holly a snappy salute. "Yes, ma'am, Captain Riley. You bet, Captain Riley. One pair of very, very big you-know-whats, coming right up."

* * *

Emily arranged the water crackers around her mother's homemade cheese ball and found the cheese spreader in the back of the silverware drawer. "Where do you want the cheese ball, Mom?"

"That can go over there on the coffee table," Patsy said distractedly as she poked a spoon into the huge casserole of cornbread and sage dressing. "Damn, this stuff needs to cook a while longer. For once I wish Mom and Dad weren't so punctual."

"Don't worry about it," Holly said as she arranged the carrots and cauliflower on a large cut glass tray. "Just put the cheese ball and veggie tray in front of Granddad and Grandma and say something nice about the Democrat of your choice and Granddad will hold forth for at least thirty minutes. And if you need a little more time you can throw in a comment or two about immigration reform."

"Really? That's all it takes?" Jason asked. "I wish we could entertain my grandparents that easily." He and Russ were busy making iced tea in Patsy's crystal tea glasses.

"Now, Holly, that's just plain mean," Russ laughed. "True, but mean. Although, in all seriousness, I think Granddad will be very interested to learn that Jimmy plans to run for Uncle Willis's bench. Where is Uncle Willis, by the way?"

"Willis called this morning. He's got a big trial starting on Monday and a lot of work to catch up on, so he decided to stay in Verde. He's having dinner tonight with Jack and Caroline," Ben said as he uncorked a bottle of Chardonnay.

"It's a shame he's not coming. Watching him and Granddad tangle is better than mud wrestling at the YWCA," Russ said.

"Yep, they don't always see eye to eye and they're not shy about saying so," Holly said.

"Hell, Judge Riley's not shy about saying anything," Jimmy huffed from his seat on the sofa. "I've been on the receiving end of one of his courtroom tirades more than once. Is Mr. Harrington just as outspoken?"

"Worse," Ben admitted. He looked from Jimmy to Jason and back to Jimmy. "Tonight should be interesting."

What do you suppose he means by that? Jason wondered as he and Jimmy exchanged a puzzled look. But the rest of the family seemed to take Ben's comment in stride.

Ben poured Jimmy his usual Scotch and soda and made Emily and Carrie non-alcoholic spritzers before pouring everyone else a glass of wine. They were nice people, Jason thought as Emily smeared some of the cheese ball on a cracker and handed it to him. Ben and Patsy had gone out of their way to make Jimmy feel comfortable today, and each of them had made it a point to thank Jason for helping and complimented him on his handling of the crisis. Jason had to admit that it felt good to help his old commanding officer, to feel like he had contributed to the welfare of a fellow wounded warrior. It felt especially good since the Rileys seemed to appreciate his handling of the emergency.

Now, if they could just accept him as a husband to Emily.

But it wasn't Mr. and Mrs. Riley he was worried about at the moment. It was Emily who had him concerned. Although the tension between them had eased somewhat during the long afternoon of helping Patsy get her huge dinner on the table, Jason could tell that Emily was troubled and withdrawn. And, as hard as he tried to shake the notion, he couldn't help but think she was keeping something from him.

The doorbell rang just as Jason and Russ delivered the last of the iced tea glasses to the table. "We'll get it," Russ called out as he motioned for Jason to come to the door with him. He looked at Jason mischievously. "Are you ready for this?"

Jason pointed to his face. "Has anybody warned them?"

"Mom probably said something when she told them about your support group. Don't worry about it. You're not going to give anybody a heart attack." Russ threw open the front door to a small crowd waiting patiently on the front porch. "Come in, come in. Dad's pouring wine, Mom's fretting about the dressing and both my sisters brought home their sweeties this year so Granddad has somebody new to fuss at."

A tiny woman with snow-white hair and Patsy's facial features bustled in. "Oh, dear, does Patsy need any help? I told her I'd make the dressing but she insisted on doing it herself." She stopped in front of Jason and offered her hand. "I'm Beatrice Harrington, and you must be Jason. We'll visit later but I need to go help Patsy with the dressing."

Jason nodded to Mrs. Harrington and then turned to face the stern-faced old man who'd just stepped through the door. Even stooped with age, Sheldon Harrington was still taller than Ben or Russ, and his carriage and demeanor was that of a man used to the world pretty much doing things his way. His face was carved in what looked like a permanent scowl and his expression didn't soften in the least when Russ introduced him to Jason.

"So you're the one Emily brought home," he said as he looked Jason up and down.

"Yes, sir," Jason said politely, not sure what to make of the old man's perusal. "I'm glad to meet you."

The old man nodded curtly and followed his wife into the big family room. "Okay, now the hard part's over," Russ said cheerfully as a middle-aged man and a younger couple carrying a couple of children trooped in. "Kevin, Tess, Uncle Shell, this is Emily's boyfriend, Jason Donahue. My Uncle Shell, my cousin Kevin Harrington, his wife Tess and their rug rats K.J. and Tina."

Shell Harrington extended his hand. "I'm glad to meet you. I'm so glad you and Emily weren't hurt any worse than you were by that madman."

"We are, too. Glad to meet you, sir. And you must be Russ's childhood partner in crime," he said to the younger man. "Emily's told me a lot about you."

Kevin made a face. "Uh-oh."

The woman shifted the little girl in her arms. "I'm glad to meet you. If I can, I'd like to get you off in a corner and pick your brain later in the evening. My brother was hurt over there and is thinking about starting a support group here in San Antonio. He's already talked to Holly, but I figure the more he knows going in the better."

"I'd be delighted."

The little boy looked at Jason. "What's wrong with your face?"

Jason could feel the adults flinch. "Hush, K.J.," Kevin said quickly. "There's nothing wrong with his face." Both young parents looked mortified.

"It's okay," Jason said quietly. "K.J., I got hurt in the war. It's kind of like I have a great big ouchie there."

"Oh. Okay." K.J. jumped out of Kevin's arms.

"I am so sorry," Tess said.

Jason held up his hand. "No need. At least he didn't run away screaming like some children have." He turned to K.J. and smiled. "Does Uncle Russ take you 'airborne' yet?"

"Oh, you bet," Russ said as he reached for the child. "Come here, rug rat, and we'll go airborne."

The Harringtons were already seated on the sofa beside Jimmy with drinks in their hands when the rest of the family tumbled in.

"So you're running for that scoundrel Willis's bench," Mr. Harrington said to Jimmy.

"Yes, sir, I am," Jimmy agreed. He leaned over and put cheese spread on a cracker.

"Don't know why you'd want to do that," Harrington huffed. "Why you would want to stay in a backwater town like Verde is beyond me. I thought you had your sights set on a Congressional seat."

Jimmy shifted uncomfortably. "I pulled out of that race on the advice of my doctors. It's going to be awhile before I'm able to carry out a Congressional campaign. Besides, I got an up-close and personal look at big-time politics and decided I don't lie skillfully enough to pull it off."

"God, what an indictment of that West Texas oil money machine," Shell said before looking abashed. "Sorry, Holly. Didn't mean to insult your mother and her friends."

"You didn't," Holly said dryly.

"Hmmph. You may have a point there, Jimmy. But Verde?" Mr. Harrington persisted. "Why Verde, of all places?"

"Maybe because he has a thriving practice, a nice house on the lake and a family ranch in Verde?" Holly asked lightly. "And I have a job there, too?" She turned to Jimmy, her eyes dancing. "Better watch it, Jimmy. In about five minutes he's going to offer you a job at Harrington, Harrington and Riley." She winked at her grandfather. "And he wouldn't even have to go to law school first, would he, Granddad?"

"And what's so amusing about that, young lady?" Harrington demanded. "I sure could use the young man in the firm." Pointing his crooked forefinger at Holly, he blasted, "I could use *you* in the firm. I could use every damn one of my grandchildren in the firm. The Harrington law firm has been in existence for a hundred and twenty-five years and is an institution in this city. We need your generation to step up to the plate so I can retire someday. So far the only two who have are Kevin and Tess."

"Hear, hear, let's drink to Kevin and Tess," Russ said as Kevin and Tess stood up and took a bow.

Everyone but Mr. Harrington laughed. His face sobering, Jimmy turned to the indignant old man. "Mr. Harrington, you just paid me the highest of compliments and for that I thank you. But my life and my work are in Verde, and I really would like to follow Judge Riley on that bench, if the voters will have me. But thank you again for thinking so highly of me."

The old man looked slightly mollified. *Smooth, Jimmy*, Jason thought. *Very smooth.*

Harrington then turned from Jimmy and nailed Russ with a glare. "And what about you, whippersnapper? You're not in the Army anymore. There's not a thing stopping you from going to law school. Why haven't you?"

"Probably because it wouldn't leave him enough time to chase every skirt in the county," Ben said acerbically.

Russ's face darkened. "Or maybe because I'd rather chase criminals and women than my tail in a high rise. And you both already know that. Look Granddad, you have Kevin and Tess, and you have a city full of hungry young lawyers who would cut off their right arm to go to work for you. You don't need me."

"Don't nag, Sheldon," Beatrice admonished. "Russ has never had any interest in the firm. None of Patsy's children have, and that's *all right*." She patted his arm. "Russ is right. There are plenty of young lawyers out there who would love to join the firm."

"But I don't want just anybody," Harrington said. "I want *family*." He turned to Emily and nailed her with a stare. "And what about you, Miss Priss? It's not too late to change your major."

"No way, Granddad," Emily laughed. "I'm going to come up with a cure for diabetes." She made a production of scanning the room. "Okay, you've fussed at every one of us now. Can we talk about something else?"

Clearly, they didn't take the old man seriously, Jason thought as Ben and Jimmy skillfully steered the conversation to the merits and drawbacks of the local Congressional candidates. Interesting family dynamics. Still, as the canapés disappeared and the conversation flowed on, he couldn't help but notice the speculative glances Mr. Harrington sent his way. Presumably, because he and Emily were not officially engaged, his future as a member of the family law firm had been left out of the discussion, but he had a feeling that Harrington would have something to say either to him or about him also before the evening was out.

Patsy finally declared the dressing cooked. Ben made quick work of carving the turkey, and soon the lavish dinner was spread out buffet-style on an elaborate piece of furniture.

Dining table conversation was sparse for a few minutes as the hungry family enjoyed Patsy's turkey and dressing, green-bean casserole and black-eyed peas. The speculative glances from Mr. Harrington continued, and Jason felt himself getting more and more uneasy as he ate. What was the old man thinking? Was he planning to lob one of his zingers Jason's way, or was he just curious as to what his granddaughter saw in a badly scarred veteran?

Finally the conversation started rolling again when Holly asked to see Emily's senior ring. Holly, Russ, and Emily shared their stories of their various ring dunkings. Mr. Harrington of course then had to express his opinion, which was that he'd never heard of anything so foolish in his life, which sent Russ, Holly, and Emily into gales of laughter. The old man looked across the table and spotted the ring on Jason's finger.

"How about you, Jason? Did you participate in this ridiculous custom as well?"

"Sure did, sir. Drank it down in record time. But I got my ring last year and didn't guzzle a whole pitcher like Russ and Holly. If I'd gotten the ring before I went into the Army I would have downed the whole pitcher like they did."

Mr. Harrington looked at Jason. "Well. I didn't realize you were that much older than Emily."

Jason felt himself stiffen as the table suddenly got quiet. "Yes, sir, I'll be thirty in a few months." He paused a moment. "I lost a few years in the hospital, Mr. Harrington. It took them awhile to put me back together after I was burned. Then I had to go back and finish my degree. I'm lucky to have found a job that allows me to finally catch up financially with my friends."

"Well, that explains it, then," Harrington said.

"Explains what, sir?"

"Why you're so interested in Emily. She and that money of hers could go a long way toward helping you catch up financially, as you put it."

Jason felt the blood drain from his head as he saw Patsy's lips tighten and Ben's head pop up. Emily exchanged a frantic look with her sister.

"I-I'm sorry, sir," Jason stammered. "What did you say?"

"I said that Emily and that money of hers could go a long way."

Jason stared at the old man for a long silent minute. "*What money, Mr. Harrington?*"

"Oh, don't be ridiculous, young man. The trust fund. The Harrington trust fund. She's bound to have told you about it."

Jason could feel his insides turning to ice. Emily had money of her own, a lot of it, from the way her grandfather was acting. His mind raced as the truth he'd been trying to ignore hit him smack in the face. *Emily was rich. She had her own money. She didn't need him to take care of her.*

Determined to shake off his shock, he lifted his chin and looked the old man in the eye. "I didn't know Emily had a trust fund. She's never mentioned it to me." He glared at Emily across the table. "You've never said a word, Emily. *Have you?*"

Emily lifted her chin and stared right back at him. "No, I haven't." She turned to her grandfather. "He didn't know, Granddad. I never told him about it. The topic never came up."

Harrington looked from Emily to Jason. "The topic never came up. And I guess it never occurred to you that she's a Harrington, either, did it, Jason? Why, everybody in San Antonio knows what it means to be a Harrington."

Jason could feel the pressure building behind his eyes. "No, sir, as it happens I'm not from San Antonio and don't know what it means to be a Harrington. Exactly what are you saying?"

"Ranching, cattle, and oil money," Holly said.

"Two banks and a law firm," Kevin added.

"Pressure and expectations," Russ said darkly.

"And a trust fund," Jimmy said speculatively. "You got one too, Holly?"

"Nope. I'm not a Harrington," Holly said cheerfully.

"Aw, damn," Jimmy winked.

"But Russ does."

Jason looked at Mr. Harrington and took a deep breath. So they all thought he was a gold digger. No wonder Ben had been so suspicious. They thought Jason was chasing Emily for her money, when nothing could be further from the truth.

Jason felt the insult burn deep in his gut. All he wanted was to take care of Emily, and they thought all he wanted was for Emily to take care of him. Jason glanced over at Emily as another horrible suspicion crossed his mind. Did she suspect him of that, too? Is that why she hadn't said anything?

He willed himself to remain at least outwardly calm as he struggled to figure out what to say next. No way was he going to let this go. He was going to set Mr. Harrington straight and Ben Riley, too, even if it made them both angry. Making a good impression on Emily's family didn't matter anymore, since he doubted he would ever be a part of it.

"No, Mr. Harrington, I'd never heard about the Harrington dynasty before and truly didn't know until just now what being a Harrington means. I didn't know about Emily's money, and to be honest with you I don't think I need it. I am perfectly willing and able to get out there and earn my own. I have a good job on the showroom floor of Blakely Chevrolet in College Station, where I put in twelve-hour shifts on a regular basis and bring home a paycheck that, while it may not be up to Harrington or Riley standards, looks pretty good to me. So, no, I have not been courting your granddaughter for her trust fund."

Mr. Harrington sat back in his chair. "Well, then. I'm sorry if I've offended you."

"I'm not the one you need to apologize to," Jason said quietly. "Emily is a lovely young woman and worth so much more than her bank balance, don't you think?"

"Well put, Jason," Russ said. "And I'm sure our grandfather knows that. Don't you, Granddad?"

Mr. Harrington's eyes widened and he turned a deep shade of red. "Of course, of course. Gracious, I never meant…"

"It's all right, Granddad," Emily murmured. "Don't worry about it."

Ben came in with a quick change of subject and Patsy and the women vanished into the kitchen to get dessert. Jason sat silent, mentally kicking himself for his stupidity. Of course Emily would have money. Any family who could afford a mansion like this was bound to have money, several generations of it.

He cringed inwardly as he thought about the boasting to Ben and Patsy about the money he was making at Blakely's. It probably was pin money to them.

The million-dollar question: Why hadn't Emily said anything? Why hadn't she been honest with him? Why had she let him go on and on about how well he was doing, when she could buy and sell him ten times over? Why had she left him in the dark? Surely she'd figured out that he was thinking in terms of a future with her.

He glanced up at her pale, set face as she brought in a couple of plates with pie and ice cream. As she handed them to Kevin and Tess, Jason felt anger shake him to his soul. No, he didn't know why she hadn't been completely honest with him. He didn't know what had prompted her to keep the money a secret, but he sure as hell intended to find out. Not tonight. He was too angry to be rational and he knew it. But at some point, Miss Emily Louise Riley was going to sit down and tell him exactly why she had not told him the truth.

* * *

Emily dried the last of the pots in the drainer and put it in its usual spot in the cabinet. She, Holly, and Tess had shooed Patsy out of the kitchen once the leftovers were put away and had cleaned up the rest of the kitchen by themselves. Tess's presence had provided a convenient buffer between Emily and the conversation she *so* didn't want to have with Holly, who had spent the rest of the evening shooting 'I told you so' looks in Emily's direction. Patsy had sent a few disapproving glances her way, but it was Jason's reaction that had her most worried. He had been visibly stunned when her grandfather dropped his little bombshell. She had to hand it to him; he rallied and put her grandfather and her father soundly in their places. Since then, he had said almost nothing to her or anyone else and he disappeared instead of watching the last of the A&M football game with the rest of the men.

Holy crap, the looks he sent her way would have scorched the asphalt off the highway. Anyone could see he was furious about being blindsided by her old curmudgeon of a grandfather. And, apparently, he was every bit as angry with her.

And she deserved it.

Not willing to face him yet, Emily perched on a barstool where she would see the game on her father's big-screen television, but she couldn't concentrate on the game to save her life. Stalling, she dreaded the upcoming talk with Jason. She'd waited too long. She should have talked to him already, and now he'd found out about the trust fund in the worst way possible.

Taking a deep breath, she pulled her shit together then went upstairs to look for him. When she couldn't find him anywhere, she came back downstairs and slipped out the side door. Not finding him out on the patio, she was about to go back inside when she spotted someone sitting in one of the folding chairs out by the basketball court. It had to be him sitting by himself in the dark.

Emily slipped across the yard and into the vacant chair beside him. He turned to face her with an unfathomable expression on his face. "Might have been nice if you'd said something, like, I don't know, three months ago."

Emily swallowed. "I'm sorry Granddad pulled that kind of stunt at the dinner table. That was low, even for him."

"He just said what your dad's thinking."

Emily shook her head. "No, that's not what Daddy's thinking. I'm not sure that's even what Granddad's thinking. He just wanted to get your goat."

"Well, he got it all right. Let's insult the granddaughter's new boyfriend between the main course and dessert. Liven up dinner if nothing else. Pretty damned shitty of the old bastard."

"I know, and I am really, really sorry he embarrassed you like that. And although I didn't deserve it, thanks for standing up for me," Emily added softly. "That meant a lot." She shifted in the chair. "I hate that you found out about the money that way."

"So how did you want me to find out about it?" he asked bitterly. "On the prenuptial agreement, maybe, down in the fine print?"

"I was going to talk to you about the trust fund," Emily protested. "Really. I still want to tell you about it."

"Too damned late for that," he bit out. "Just how much is that trust fund of yours worth, anyway?"

Emily gulped. "I'm not sure."

"Ballpark it," Jason snapped.

"The last time I looked it was four-million-five."

Emily could hear the swift intake of Jason's breath. "Well, damn. *Damn.* Damn it to hell."

"Jason, it…"

"Shut up, Emily." His voice was velvet steel. "Just shut up."

"Jason…"

"I said *shut up.* I am not going to talk to you about this right now. I am not going to discuss this under your mother's roof where we might be overheard. We will talk once we get back to College Station." He shoved himself out of the chair and walked off before she could say another word.

Emily sensed more than embarrassment, more than anger at being blindsided and insulted at the dinner table—those she expected and understood. Something else was going on with Jason. Every other man in America would've been genuinely happy to find out that she was rich.

Not Jason.

He got more pissed off when she told him how much was in the trust fund. Even though he didn't need her money and, bravo for him, had told her grandfather so, Jason put a lot of store in the almighty dollar. Why was he infuriated to learn she had a boatload in the bank?

Chapter Seven

Jason stared up at the ceiling and then over at the clock on the bedside table. It was almost three in the morning and he was no closer to going to sleep than he had been when he hit the bed close to midnight. He stared at the door to the connecting bathroom that opened into Emily's room. Was she awake, too? Did she even give a damn? Did she even care that it was over between them?

Maybe she didn't realize what tonight's revelations meant to their future. Or maybe she wasn't even thinking in terms of a future with him. At this point, he didn't know. But he couldn't ask her to marry him now. She didn't need him. She had her own money and a damn lot of it.

He reached up with his thumb to wipe away the tear that was leaking out of his eye. Damn it all to hell. What kind of karmic payback was this? The one thing he could have offered her, the one thing he could have given her in their marriage, the one thing that would have made marrying him worth it was the good life he meant to give her: a nice house, new cars, a comfortable existence. And, as it turned out, that was the last thing she needed from him.

Two mornings later, he put the last of his and Emily's suitcases in the car and slammed the back shut with a little more force than necessary. Thank God the weekend was nearly over. He'd run out of phony smiles and polite conversation and was tired of making nice when all he wanted to do was beat holes in a sheetrock wall.

Determined not to ruin Patsy's house party, both he and Emily had presented a united front to the rest of the family and behaved perfectly toward one another in the presence of others. But on the few occasions they were alone, the strain between them was thick enough to cut with a knife. Jason made no effort to hide his anger from Emily and she was strangely defiant, as though he were to blame for the tension between them.

Bullshit. This was on her. No way had he done anything wrong.

Jason squinted at the too-bright sun, cursing the demon on his shoulder last night that had prompted him to sit around with Russ and Jimmy in the garage apartment until three in the morning, consuming Jimmy's favorite Scotch and shooting the bull with them on just about every topic imaginable. Except, that is, what was really bothering him. In spite of the tongue-loosening power of expensive whiskey, Jason had not breathed a word to Jimmy or Russ about the argument with Emily or the guaranteed demise of their relationship, even when the discussion turned to damned-if-I-can-understand-women.

The hurt cut too deep.

Even if the relationship was over, he intended to ask why she kept the trust fund a secret. She owed him the truth. It would be interesting, if nothing else, to hear what she had to say about her secrecy in the face of something as significant as four–and-a-half-million dollars.

Jason locked the car and spotted Holly dragging a couple of large suitcases across the circular driveway. "Here, let me get those for you," he said as he relieved her of the suitcases and put them in the back of the Navigator. "About ready to go?"

"No thanks to Jimmy," Holly groused. "Good Lord, how much did the three of you put away during your late-night bullshit session? He's upstairs gulping coffee with his headache pills and muttering something about you clowns drinking him under the table."

"Damned if that's so," Jason snorted. "That good lawyer of yours can hold his booze just fine, thank you very much. And so can your brother."

"Well, did you three get all the problems of the world settled?"

"Oh, absolutely. Drought in Texas, peace in the Middle East, drug trafficking in South America, worldwide nuclear disarmament. All done."

"And what about Emily and Jason? Did you get that one solved, too?"

Jason shot Holly a go-to-hell look. "That one's not ever going to be solved, and I'll be damned if I'm going to talk about it with either one of *them*."

Holly's eyes narrowed. "And just why wouldn't you want to talk about it with either of *them*?"

"Jimmy the Rich and Russ the Richer?" Jason rolled his eyes. "The small-town prince and the trust-fund baby? Do you think either of them would have a clue?" He stopped and took a deep breath. "I feel like a damned fool for ever thinking Emily and I belonged together. She doesn't need me. The one thing I thought I could give her is the one thing she absolutely, positively doesn't need."

"You obviously haven't grown those balls yet, have you?" Holly asked quietly, the compassion in her eyes a contrast to the sarcasm of her question.

"You knew," Jason said suddenly. "You knew Emily and the rest of them were loaded. Why didn't you tell me and not let me make a fool of myself in front of the whole damn family?"

"And rip away the self-confidence you were finally achieving with the job and the generous commissions? Jason, I didn't care if you were making a fool of yourself in front of the whole damn world. You needed to blow your own horn a little. I knew that, and so did Emily. For God's sake, talk to her. And I mean talk, not just scream at her in anger. *Please*."

Jason inclined his head. "I'll talk to her, Holly. For all the good it will do."

Holly shook her head and disappeared inside the house. The front door banged open a moment later and Emily came down the steps, followed by Ben and Patsy.

"Ready to go?" Jason asked as Emily tossed her handbag into the front seat.

"As ready as I'll ever be," she said brightly. She hugged both of her parents. "I love you, Mom. I love you, Daddy."

The Rileys released Emily and Jason offered his hand to Patsy. "Thank you for a lovely Thanksgiving," he said, forcing warmth into his words. It wasn't Patsy's fault the holiday had gone south.

"Handshake, poo," she said as she engulfed Jason in a huge hug. "Thank you for coming. We loved having you."

Jason released Patsy and offered his hand to Ben. "Thank you for having me, sir."

Ben shook Jason's hand. "Thank you for bringing Emily home to see us." He looked Jason square in the eye. "You seem like a fine young man. Thank you for being so good to my daughter."

"You're welcome, Mr. Riley," Jason said quietly. As an endorsement went, from a man like Ben Riley it was probably a good one. But it was a moot point now.

Jason and Emily climbed in the car and she waved to her parents, smiling and waving until the car turned the corner. Then she dropped all pretense of friendliness.

"I presume you want to wait until we get back to College Station to talk about things?" she said coolly.

"You presume right. I'll be damned if I try to talk to you while I fight this damn holiday traffic."

Emily nodded, sent a glare his way then pulled her Kindle out of her large handbag, leaving him to duck and dodge in the swarming streets and highways between San Antonio and College Station.

It was going to be a long trip.

* * *

Emily looked up from the Kindle she had been pretending to read for the last three hours and gritted her teeth. They were almost back at College Station and the discussion Emily had to admit was long overdue. But she'd had a weekend to think about the situation, too. She had her reasons for not telling Jason about the money, even if no one else agreed with them, and Jason was just going to have to understand. She'd be damned if she would apologize for protecting her own interests for once and refusing to be seen as another man's gravy train.

They pulled up in front of the duplex and without speaking brought the luggage in. Emily started tossing her dirty clothes in a pile while Jason stood there watching. Emily could feel the tension ratcheting up between them, but if Jason wanted to talk he was damn well going to start the conversation himself.

"Now that we're out from under your mother's roof, would you care to explain things to me?" Jason finally demanded.

"Sure. What would you like me to explain?"

He snorted. "Sorta obvious, Em. But okay, I'll play. Let's start with why you let me make a fool of myself bragging in front of your parents about my job and all the damn money I thought I was making when you know it's chicken feed to people like them."

"People like them? Jason, my mother taught school and Daddy was a country lawyer until Granddad hired him. They know about hard work and they know the value of a dollar."

"They also live in a mansion and know what a lot of money looks like from looking at their own, and they know damn well I'm nowhere in their ballpark," he said bitterly.

"My parents aren't like that," Emily said sharply. "Besides, it wasn't them that brought up your new job, it was you. You were the one who tooted your own horn until your face was red."

"I had to give them something to respect, didn't I?" he shot back. "After all, the first time they met me I was a disfigured loser who couldn't even get a job until your sister went to bat for me. I just wanted them to know that I was doing better. You should have told me. You should have told me that my two-bit job wasn't anywhere near being in the Harrington-Riley league and wasn't going to impress them one damned bit."

"There is nothing two-bit about your job. Damn it, I was proud of you. I was proud you were getting out there and making a success of yourself in a damn tough business. My bad."

"All right. You let me make an ass of myself because you were proud of me. Not that I buy it, but, for argument's sake, let's say you're telling the truth. This time." He ran his hand over his head. "Wanna tell me why in the hell, in all the months we've been together, you haven't said a word about the trust fund? What was the big fuckin' secret?"

Cornered, Emily shut down. "In the beginning it was flat-out none of your business. I don't share personal things like that with acquaintances."

"Really? And later? When we were more than acquaintances? Like maybe when I was sleeping in your bed and letting you plan the house I wanted to build and dropping marriage hints thick on the ground? What about then?"

She lifted her chin and looked him in the eye. "I was waiting until you asked me to marry you. I was waiting until you had declared your love and put a ring on my finger."

Jason didn't even try to hide his contempt. "So you weren't even going to tell me the truth about the money until I proposed? You were going to lie to me until then?"

"I didn't *lie* to you; I just didn't tell you everything," she snapped. "And yeah, I was going to wait until then."

"Why?"

"I have my reasons."

"Which I presume you're not interested in sharing. Again. So what else haven't you told me?" he demanded. "What else have you been lying to me about?"

"Nothing," Emily ground out. "Not one damned thing."

"And you expect me to believe that? How damn dumb do you think I am?"

"All right then, what have I been lying about?"

"How about the scars, Emily? Been lying about those? Oh, hey, Jason, maybe your ugly damned face and the scars do too matter. Maybe I do care and I'm just lying to make you feel better about yourself. Or, better yet, maybe I do care and picked you on purpose because you're an ugly bastard and won't cheat on me like that pretty boy did. How about it, Emily? Any of that sound anywhere near the truth?"

She looked at Jason's dejected face and felt her self-righteousness collapse. Every bone in her body hurt and years of hiding from herself crashed against her ribcage, robbing her of breath. Long moments hung between them before her mettle allowed her to go on.

"Oh my God. Do you really think I would lie to you about that? Do you really think I would deliberately choose you because you're disfigured?" But it made sense, she admitted to herself as she cringed inwardly. In Jason's shoes, with Jason's insecurities, she would have come to exactly the same conclusion. "It's not true, Jason, honestly, and I'm sorry my actions made you think a thing like that."

He didn't say a word, just stared as if he didn't believe a thing she said.

Deep breath. Truth time.

"You want the truth? Really. Honestly. Here's the truth. I never lied about your looks. Your looks have nothing to do with how I feel about you. Never have. I didn't tell you about the money cuz you flat-out told me that a person's bank balance is sometimes the most important thing about them. You judge everybody, including yourself, by their money or lack of it. That's your yardstick. Nothing about the person, just their money. I didn't want you to marry me *because you fell in love with mine*."

Jason stood frozen as Emily looked at him in horror. She had wounded him and hadn't meant to.

"You think I'm a gold digger," he said finally, hurt and anger glittering in his eyes. "You think that money would make you more attractive to me. You think I'd marry you because of your money."

"It seemed in the realm of possibility."

"*Damn* you." Jason said bitterly. "Damn you for even thinking such a thing. You're no better than your grandfather."

She lifted her chin a bit. "Jason, look at my track record," she said softly. It's happened to me not once but twice. Twice, Jason. In the past, I had been honest about the money then found out the money was all they wanted. You asked about Brandon?" She shook her head. "He was marrying me for my money. The afternoon I caught him in bed with that other girl? He told me in one-syllable words that the money was the only reason he'd marry me. That *killed,* and it still does nearly a year and a half after the fact. You say I'm no better than my grandfather and maybe I'm not. But how in the hell can I trust my own judgment after being taken not once but twice? How was I supposed to know whether or not you were going to be any better than Jeff or Brandon if I told you about the money? How was I supposed to know you weren't doing the same thing? Was I so horrible, so wrong not to want that to happen a third time? Was I so damn wrong for wanting to be loved for who I am, not what I have?"

"Am I so damn wrong for being thoroughly pissed at you for even thinking I'm like either one of those bastards?" Jason roared back.

His lack of compassion pushed her to a different place. "With your love of the green stuff? What in the hell was I supposed to think? Yes, you're wrong. You gave me every damn reason to doubt you and now you're angry because I did."

"All right then. Listen and listen close, Emily, so maybe you won't doubt this. Yes, I've been obsessed with money. Yes, I've busted my ass to earn a lot of it and yes, I've been proud of myself for bringing it home with me at the end of the week. You know why? For *you*, damn it. I wanted to give it to you. I wanted to do nice things for you. I wanted to be able to offer you something in a husband besides an older guy with an ugly damned face. That's the only reason I gave a shit about the money. So I could take decent care of you." He turned to face the door then turned back. "But you already have so damn much money you can't even appreciate it." He jerked up the house plans and thrust them at her. "I won't need these any more. I was building it for you."

Emily watched, stunned and silent, as Jason unloaded his drawers and threw his clothes into a couple of large duffels and a laundry basket. He made quick work of gathering up the rest of his possessions then unsnapped her apartment key from his key ring, laid it on the dresser, and tossed the duffels and laundry basket onto the front porch.

It was over. He was taking his things and leaving. He tossed his laptop and phone chargers into a case and set them outside the door. He made a final quick sweep through the small apartment then his eyes landed on Emily, sitting stone still on the bed.

"We weren't meant to be. Maybe the next one will appreciate what I want to do for her."

Emily's eyes narrowed. "Don't forget to run a financial report before you get in too deep. You'll want to make sure she's poor enough to fit your criteria."

Jason jerked open the front door and slammed it behind him.

Damn him anyway, she thought as the tears she'd held back leaked down her cheeks. How in the hell had it gone so terribly, horribly wrong? She'd gauged her future based on her past. Cautious but smart, right? Apparently not.

She sure as hell didn't know what she could do to fix things between them, and after the things they said—their emotions rubbed raw—she wasn't even sure she wanted to try.

* * *

Jason clicked on the coffee maker then started making his usual circle of folding chairs. He didn't want to be here tonight and had almost called his wounded warriors and cancelled the meeting. But he had no excuse for not wanting to come other than his fight with Emily and his bitter disappointment that his hopes for a future with her had gone up in dollar signs. It wouldn't have been fair to the others to cancel just because he was torn up inside, so the meeting would go on as planned, and if he was just going through the motions? That was about all he'd been doing since Sunday, and there was no reason to expect this evening to be any different.

He plastered on a smile and forced himself to stand at the door and greet his support group the way he always did, shaking their hands and gauging their moods by the subtle signs he'd learn to interpret on the sales floor at Blakely's. Hillary, pinch-faced and tense—a bad week. He hoped she would share and get it off her chest. Joel, distracted and deep in thought—probably would have something to bounce off the crowd. Zach, for once without Rosalee and seriously excited about something—maybe he'd gotten a better job? It should be an interesting meeting.

Jason thought about what he would say when it was his turn to talk. Should he tell them he and Emily were no longer together? No, It would lead to why, and the trust fund was Emily's business and hers alone. More to the point, the whole episode was just too painful to air, even in front of his friends.

The group got coffee and settled in and Jason started the ball rolling. "How was everybody's Thanksgiving?" he threw out to the group.

"Lousy," Hillary said. "My mom invited my dumbshit cousins who thought it would be funny to set off a string of firecrackers right behind me and I freaked and tried to choke one of them. So now my aunt's not speaking to my mom, my mom's not speaking to me, and my dad reamed my mom out for inviting them in the first place. Now my mom and my dad are not speaking to each other."

"Must have been nice and quiet for the rest of the weekend," Joel quipped. "I wish Karen and her family would try that."

Hillary and Karen both shot Joel a go-to-hell look. "How about you, Joel? How was yours?" Jason asked.

"Interesting. I talked to Karen's doctor brother about going to medical school, and he's about convinced me to try for physician's assistant school instead."

Jason tilted his chair back while the other group members looked at each other and Joel. "Why?" Hillary demanded. "That was a little mean of him."

"Doesn't he think an amputee can cut it in med school?" Jason added.

"No, he wasn't being mean and he thinks I could cut med school just fine. But he said if I really wanted to provide primary medical care to people, the PA route was the way to go. He said that doctors don't do that anymore. My legs or lack of them has nothing to do with it."

The discussion then veered to health care, a subject unfortunately dear to every member of Jason's group, and then on to other things. Their allotted time went quickly and Jason was about to close the meeting and send everybody home when Zach tentatively raised his hand.

"Yeah, Zach?" Jason asked.

Zach smiled and took a ring box out of his jacket pocket. *Oh, no,* Jason thought as Zach opened the box and showed the group a small but beautifully designed engagement ring, its center stone sparkling even under the harsh fluorescent lighting. "I-m g-gonna p-propose to Rosalee," he said, beaming from ear to ear. "I-I'm gonna ask her S-Saturday night."

And she is going to say 'no,' Jason thought, cringing inwardly for the misguided young man holding the pretty little ring. The one-time pre-med major's closed-head injury was severe, leaving him with crippling aphasia, so it was difficult for him to speak, and impairing him to the point that he could barely read a newspaper. He was currently working as a custodian and there was doubt that he would ever be capable of much more than that. Rosalee loved Zach, but more than once she had quietly expressed concern about what the future held for the two of them.

Zach was going to be so disappointed. No way was Rosalee going to say yes to spending the rest of her life with a man who, however much he loved her, had so little he could offer her at this point. His heart sinking for Zach, Jason nevertheless ooh-ed and aah-ed along with the rest of them at the pretty little ring. They clapped and shook Zach's hand and razzed him a little with marriage jokes, and if any of the support group members shared Jason's private doubts, they certainly weren't letting them be known. Still, after the meeting was over and Zach was helping Jason stack the chairs, Jason felt like he had to do something to prepare Zach for Rosalee's probable rejection.

"So, Zach, does Rosalee know you plan to propose to her this weekend?"

Zach shook his head. "I w-want to s-s..." He gathered his thoughts for a minute. "Surprise her. S-Saturday night. Fancy r-r-Fancy steak. Ring." He grinned wickedly. "Good s-sex later."

God, this was getting worse and worse. "Zach, have you really and truly thought this through? Carefully? Are you sure this is what you want to do? What if..." Jason trailed off helplessly, not sure how he could gently voice his doubts.

Zach's smile faded. "S-She might s-say 'no.' I g-get that. B-but I l-love her and think th-that will be enough." He touched his chest with his hand. "F-faith. I have f-faith."

Tears shimmered in Jason's eyes as he watched Zach walk out the door. Zach was going to get hurt Saturday night, he thought as he folded the last of the chairs and washed out the coffee pot. The poor man, who had already lost so much, was going to be losing that much more. Because no way a woman like Rosalee—who had so much to offer and who was already disappointed in the way things were turning out for her and Zach—was going to be willing to spend the rest of her life with a man who had so little to give back to her.

Sound familiar?

Chapter Eight

Jason trudged up the steps and let himself in his side of the duplex. It was almost ten at night, but he had worked the afternoon-to-evening shift, snagged a last-minute sale then had dickered with the customer for almost an hour before settling on a price and writing a contract. After, he'd had to wait in a line of cars at the fast-food window for his tacos.

He had sold five cars already this week and was on his way to being number one salesman of the month again, but somehow his success had lost its sweetness and now he was working to pay the bills and pad his bank account.

Ever since the revelations during Thanksgiving weekend and the realization that, no matter how hard he worked, he would never reach the Harrington family's level of financial success, he had been forced to take another look at his goals and dreams. He needed to quit measuring himself solely by a financial yardstick and start looking at the other things he could accomplish and perhaps was already accomplishing, like helping his fellow wounded warriors. Yeah, he still cared about the money and to some extent always would, but making a lot of it was not going to be the answer to all his problems.

And it sure wasn't going to be the answer with Emily.

Apparently she too realized the futility of their relationship, because she'd made no attempt to contact him since their fight. Except for one glimpse of her Wednesday morning as she was getting into her car, he hadn't even seen her.

He missed her.

He missed her smile, her laughter, and Lord, did he miss the way she wrapped her long, strong legs around his hips when they made love. He even missed the way she rubbed the moisturizing lotion on his scarred skin. Damn, he thought for the thousandth time, why couldn't she have needed him just a little?

Benny's door was open and his room was quiet, and Jason could hear the faint sound of country music coming from behind Wade's closed door. He poured a glass of milk, sat down at the table and flicked on the television. "Geez, turn it down, will ya?" Benny called out. "I'm trying to study."

"And I'm trying to eat," Jason replied churlishly. "Shut your damned door."

"I don't want to shut my damned door; it gets too hot in here. Just turn the damned thing down a little."

Jason picked up the remote and turned the volume up two more notches. Ignoring the curses coming out of Benny's room, he unwrapped his tacos and had taken his first bite when Benny, clad only in boxers and an old T-shirt, stomped into the room and yanked the plug out of the wall.

"Look, you may not have to study for a shit-pile of finals but Wade and I sure do, and I would sincerely appreciate a little peace and quiet in which to do it. So would you please yank the cob out of your ass and quit taking your fight with Emily out on Wade and me before I knock you on your ugly damned ass? And don't think I won't. I've had enough of the shitty attitude you've had since you moved back in."

"Shove it up your ass, Keller. I pay a third of the rent and I kept paying it when I was at Emily's and I'll play the TV as damned loud as I feel like," Jason snapped. "Plug it back in."

Benny threw down the plug and turned his back. Jason stood up and whirled him back around to face him and was suddenly rewarded with Benny's fist landing smack in the middle of his face. Jason stumbled backward and threw up his fist to retaliate but froze when Wade's door flew open and Wade let loose with an ear-splitting whistle.

"Time out, you clowns. You get in a fight and you'll be buying a lot of trashed furniture I ain't helping you pay for. So chill, damn it."

Jason took a step backward and so did Benny.

"That's better," Wade said. "Tacos smell good, Jason. Don't you think you better eat them before they get cold, or one of your hungry roommates snatches them?"

His appetite suddenly gone, Jason stared at the tacos with distaste. "You can have the damn things. I'm going to bed."

"Okay, that's it," Wade said. "A fistfight's no big deal, but you wouldn't give us your tacos unless something pretty serious was going on. Sit yourself down, asshole and tell us why you've been worse than a bear with a sore paw."

Jason glared at Wade, who glared right back. "Sit. Down. Now." Wade pointed at the chair Jason had vacated while Wade and Benny sat down in two others. "Now, if I didn't know better I would say that your ever-present evil temper these days has something to do with the fact that you have moved back in with us and that you have not spoken one word to our lovely red-headed neighbor for the better part of the week. How'm I doing?"

Jason shrugged and picked up his taco. "It's over with her. I'm giving Mom back my grandmother's ring."

Benny and Wade didn't try to hide their surprise. "Over? You mean this isn't temporary? What the hell happened?" Benny pushed.

Jason looked from Benny to Wade. "You mean Emily hasn't told you the whole embarrassing story?"

Wade and Benny both shook their heads. "Not a word, man. Not that we've gone over there and asked her," Wade said. "So?"

"She lied to me. She flat-out lied to me about something really important. And then she let me embarrass myself thoroughly in front of her whole family."

Benny and Wade looked at one another. "Uh-oh," Wade said. "You found out about the trust fund."

"Christ. Even you knew," Jason said through clenched teeth. "Son of a bitch. I guess everybody in the damned world knew about that trust fund except me."

It keeps getting worse and worse.

"We've known her a lot longer than you have, man. And the only, and I repeat *only* reason we knew was cuz we had to put her back together the afternoon she caught Brandon the Bastard in bed with his lay of the day. He told Emily that her only appeal as a woman was her bank balance. Otherwise I seriously doubt that we'd know to this day."

Benny penned Jason with a stare. "She doesn't tell just anybody, you know."

"Since when was I 'just anybody'?" Jason asked coldly. "I was fucking going to ask her to marry me."

"Yeah, and the minute you fucking proposed she was going to tell you about the fucking money," Wade said. "Until then it really wasn't any of your business, now was it?"

"Just for the record, I thought she should've told you," Benny said. "My man Wade here said she was wise to wait."

"Thanks for the vote of confidence," Jason said.

"That's not quite all of it. I also said that if she didn't trust you she had no business marrying you period."

Jason looked at the two of them. "Thanks for the ringing endorsements," he said dryly. "Damn it, why did you tell her a thing like that? You guys know me pretty well, don't you?"

"Actually, we *don't* know you well enough to read you in a situation like this," Wade countered. "We've barely known you a year. Sure, you seem nice and act like you really care for Emily, but so did the other two, and we thought we knew them, too."

"Twice now Emily's been courted for her bank account," Benny added. "The first guy, Jeff Carmichaels, was more or less harmless. He came from another old-money family in San Antonio and was only doing what his family expected him to do. You know, make as financially advantageous an alliance as possible. He never said or did anything to hurt her and they parted amicably, but that second bastard, he was Carmichael's roommate and knew from Jeff that Emily was wealthy.

"He chased her big-time and she fell, and fell hard. Then when she caught him screwing around on her, she not only found out that he was only into her for the money, but he said some things that I'm not sure she's over to this day. Thanks to him, she's got some serious self-esteem issues when it comes to her looks."

"Getting called a 'paper-bag fuck' will do that, you know," Wade murmured.

"He called her a *what*?" Jason pounded the table. "I wish I'd beat the shit out of him that night in San Antonio. No wonder she reacted to him the way she did."

"Getting a clue now? By the time you entered the picture, Emily had learned to be cautious, and we'd learned to be cautious for her," Benny said. "I think her mom and sister wanted her to level with you, but Wade over here encouraged her to wait. Both of us, actually, when you started making a lot of money and wouldn't shut up about it." Benny winked. "I know it's not up to her family's standards but it sure looks like a lot of money to me."

Jason smiled faintly. "Thanks. I guess."

"Jason, she didn't tell you about the money because she wants to be loved for herself," Wade said. "She doesn't want to be loved for her money, and she doesn't want to use the money to make herself more attractive to a potential husband like a lot of less-than-gorgeous rich girls would have. I admire the hell out of her for that."

"Agreed. Ya know, I wouldn't be worried too much about being embarrassed in front of the family, including that old grandfather," Benny said. "People like that might be snotty about what they have, but they can usually appreciate the work ethic in others. It's the deadbeats that set them off."

"I hope you guys are right," Jason said.

"So will you please go next door and make up with Emily so we can stand being around you again?" Wade pleaded.

"No. Look, I appreciate all that you've shared with me tonight and I think I can understand where Emily was coming from, but just because I understand doesn't mean that we'll be getting back together. I still don't have any kind of future with her. I guess I never did."

"But...but why?" Benny asked.

"What makes you think a thing like that?" Wade added.

Jason looked at them sadly. "Because if Emily has a trust fund she doesn't need me, does she? She doesn't need what I could have offered her."

"Jason, maybe you better explain this a little better, because I don't think Wade and I are quite getting this."

"Okay, then, let me spell it out for you. I'm ten years older than Emily. I was practically burned alive in an explosion and am so damned ugly that people flinch when they look at me. I have permanent lung damage, I can't regulate my body temperature worth shit, and I can't be out in the sun.

"Gentlemen, I am no fucking bargain in the marriage market. The only, and I do mean only thing I have going for me in this life is that I am finally in a position to make a little money and offer a woman some nice things... a big house, new cars, some pretty baubles now and again. Emily Riley is the last woman in the state of Texas who needs that from a man. She can pay for her own."

Benny and Wade were silent for a minute. "So you think because you're not in the *People* Sexiest Man Alive issue the only thing you have to offer a woman is *money*?" Wade asked.

"You don't think she'd love you for yourself?" Benny added.

Jason ground his teeth together. "Myself isn't much these days, guys. I have to do a little better than that."

Benny rolled his eyes. "Hoo, boy. I don't know what the hell to say to you, man. This is way over my pay grade. But I am gonna tell you what you're about to do. You're not going to just give up on the loveliest young woman who has ever come into your life. You're going to screw up your courage, buy lots of flowers, and take your interesting-looking self next door and talk to the lady. A lovely lady who wants to be loved for herself and who, I'm betting, wants to do the same for you."

"You're going to quit dwelling on that damned face of yours," Wade added. "It's just what you look like, not who you are. And, you're going to start taking into consideration the fact that you are not the only one who feels badly about not being drop-dead gorgeous. Emily's horribly insecure about her looks since Brandon did his number on her. You need to quit focusing on your face and pay a little more attention to admiring hers."

Jason looked from one to the other. "I can talk to her. In fact, I probably should, if for no other reason than to apologize to her for the fight. But the bottom line hasn't changed, and talking to Emily isn't going to change that."

"No, it won't," Wade agreed. "But your perspective on it just might."

Chapter Nine

Emily put her groceries in the trunk of her car and swore as a carload of fraternity types, convertible top down and sound system blaring, sped through the parking lot. Damn little assholes, she thought crossly as she slammed her trunk shut. Glaring at their impudent grins, she shot them the finger and climbed behind her own wheel, cursing the traffic jam in the parking lot as students like her in the off-campus housing stocked up on enough frozen dinners and snack foods to see them through the last two weeks of the semester.

She thought ruefully of the two meager sacks of groceries she was taking home this afternoon. Now that Jason was back next door, her grocery shopping had shrunk by two-thirds. She wondered if he would take a break at Christmastime when she went to San Antonio or if he would work through the holidays, packing in as many holiday commissions as he could before sales slowed in January. Probably work, she thought cynically, or maybe not. If he'd been telling the truth, if he'd really been working so hard just to do things for her, now that they weren't a couple any more he might be willing to give it a bit of a breather.

Not her concern anymore. He had walked out of her apartment and her life. Emily forced her lips not to tremble and her eyes not to tear up. Ironic. Jeff and Brandon were courting her for her money, and Jason left her because she had too much.

As much as Emily wanted to say 'to hell with Jason' and mean it, she had to admit that she missed him: his smiles, his laughter, the way he held her in his arms and nuzzled his face against her neck as he lay sleeping beside her in the lumpy old bed. She missed it all and desperately wished that things had not turned out the way they had. But even if she had a do-over button she could push, she wasn't sure she would do anything differently. She still longed for a relationship based on love alone, and she wasn't sure that was possible with Jason.

Hell, she was beginning to wonder if it was possible with any man.

The money would always be there, no matter who she eventually ended up with. The money would always be a part of who she was. She wasn't foolish enough to wish it away, but she admitted to herself that when it came to her relationships with men, the trust fund was a damned nuisance.

She pulled into the driveway and parked beside Jason's car. What was he doing home this early? He seldom got home before eight or nine. Forcing herself not to think about his comings and goings, she unloaded the groceries and was carrying them up the porch steps when Jason opened his door and met her at the top of the stairs.

"Let me help you with those," he said as he relieved her of the heavier bag.

"Why are you home this early?" Emily asked. "Why aren't you at work?"

"I asked for the afternoon off. I wanted to talk to you. But let's get the groceries unloaded first."

He waited patiently while she unlocked the door. Then, without speaking, he unloaded the bag while Emily put away the groceries. She sneaked several peeks in his direction, wondering what he was doing here and what he was thinking, but his face was unreadable and she supposed she would just have to wait and see what he wanted to talk to her about.

The tension between them, already as taut as a bowstring, continued to ratchet up as he made a cup of coffee then loaded the coffee machine with a pod of Emily's favorite herb tea. He handed her the cup and motioned her to the living room.

"I think maybe we need to talk," he said as he sat down in the easy chair.

She sat down across from him on the sofa. "So talk."

Jason took a deep breath. "I was an ass about the trust fund and I'm sorry. Even though I still don't agree with them, I understand your reasons for not telling me about the money. It hurt, you know. Being put in the same category as those other two guys."

"I'm sorry, too. I never meant to hurt you." Tears shimmered, blurring her vision. "But you frightened me. You put such an emphasis on the money you were making, I was honestly afraid it would make a difference in how you felt about me. And I don't want it to. I want to be loved for myself, for round-faced, redheaded, diabetic Emily Riley, not because I'm a Harrington heir."

"I do love you for yourself, Em. I think I fell in love with you that day at the Fourth of July picnic, when you popped off to me and Holly made me go ask you for a date. I know I love you now."

"And I love you, too," she said softly.

Jason looked at Emily sadly. "And that makes the situation that much sadder, doesn't it?"

"What situation?" she asked. "If you love me and I love you, then what is the problem?"

"The damn money," he said. "The trust fund. That changes everything, doesn't it?"

"I'm not sure why." She stood and took a few paces. "You've made a big deal out of the trust fund without even understanding what that trust fund is all about. It's not a big fat gravy train, Jason. It's a family legacy and a responsibility that I don't take lightly."

Jason didn't try to hide his confusion. "How so?"

"That money isn't just mine to do with as I please. I have to accomplish something with it." A faint smile crossed Emily's lips. "My great-great-grandfather was obscenely wealthy and at the same time brilliantly shrewd about human nature. He knew that if he left his money to the succeeding generations with no restrictions or stipulations that he ran the risk of turning them into DOMWITs."

"What on earth is a DOMWIT?"

"A Downwardly Mobile White Inheriting a Trust. Not a very nice moniker but too true to be funny in some cases.

"He left specific instructions on how that money is to be handled. It's not for us to live on. We work to feed our faces just like the rest of the world. But by the time we're thirty or so, we are expected to have a plan to put that money to work, either as a profit-making business or a charity of some kind. And whatever we do with that money, it better be a success, whether or not it's intended to make money. Failure is not an option in the Harrington family." Emily clasped her hands in front of her. "My great-grandparents founded Harrington Saving and Loan, which does turn a profit but specializes in the banking needs of small businesses and the working man. Since Grandma Beatrice is an adoptee, Granddad and Grandma founded Happy Family Adoption Agency, which arranges more successful adoptions than any other agency in the state. Uncle Shell used his as seed money for a profitable breakfast taco chain in San Antonio, and Mom used hers to start a shelter for abused women. It will be interesting to see how Russ and Kevin use theirs. Whatever they do, it better pan out."

"And you?"

"I don't know yet. I'm thinking in terms of starting a business that designs and sells innovative diabetes accessories for young diabetics. Designer glucose monitor and insulin kits, cute clothing to house and hide insulin pumps, good-looking medic-alert jewelry, insulated traveling bags, stuff that every diabetic needs but that is either hard to come by or unattractive or both. If the money stretches far enough I might even get into training sugar-sniffing dogs." She bounced on her heels. "It might sound silly to make a cute monitor kit, but for a fifteen-year-old that has to carry one, it might mean the difference between feeling like a dork or not."

"I don't think it's silly at all. It should be quite profitable," he mused.

"It better make a little, anyway. I'm not sure it's going to make me all that rich."

"No, you're already all that rich," he said dryly.

"And that bothers you, doesn't it?" She could feel her face fall. "It isn't only that I didn't tell you about the money, is it? The fact that I have it bothers you."

"Yeah, it bothers me," he admitted.

"It still bothers you? Even knowing how I'll be using it? *Why*? Most men would be glad to find out that the woman they love has a trust fund."

"Because it means you don't need me," he said baldly. "You don't need the one thing I could offer you in this life."

Emily frowned in confusion. "I'm afraid you just lost me. What do you think it is that I don't need from you?"

"It's like this." He stood then took a step toward her. "I don't care what the poems and the songs and the love stories say about love and romance and all that shit, even when a couple loves each other dearly, a relationship between a man and a woman is a partnership, especially if that relationship is formalized into a marriage. Into that partnership each person brings what they can offer. Are you with me so far?"

"Absolutely," she said. "And for the record, I agree with that."

Jason took another step toward her. "Okay. So let's take this a bit further. Let's look at you and me. You're young, you're brilliant, you're educated, you're warm and loving and caring, and even though you have the integrity not to trade on your considerable financial assets to make yourself more attractive to a man, you do bring those assets, and the business they will eventually fund, with you to the partnership." He grinned wickedly. "You have a body to die for and are absolutely dynamite between the sheets." He reached out and framed her face in his large hands. "And you have the face of an angel, sweet Emily, even if you don't think you do." He leaned down and kissed her softly on the lips. "You have just about everything a man could want in a woman. You bring a lot to the table."

"I also bring a raging case of diabetes and all that entails," she reminded him.

"No, you bring a controlled case of diabetes that you take very good care of and that doesn't hold you back in the least."

He released her face and took a couple of steps backward. "Now let's take a look at me. I'm ten years older than you, which right now might not seem like much, but I promise you, time would catch up with us sooner or later. I was almost ten years late getting my degree and am just now getting started with my life as a working adult. I'm finally earning some money but have no assets to speak of at this point. I have scars and replacement skin over half my body and all the problems associated with those, plus my health is compromised by lung damage.

"I'm ugly, Em, seriously ugly. I can't offer you one damn thing in terms of youth or looks or physical appeal. That and most of the rest of what I could have offered you was burned off of me on a hot summer day in Baghdad almost ten years ago. When it comes to what I bring to the table, I'm not much of a bargain."

He held up his hand when she opened her mouth.

"Please, hear me out. I'm well aware of my drawbacks as a potential husband. But I love you and I desperately wanted to offer you something that would make it worth your while to marry me, something I could offer you that would make up for all the things that I can't offer you due to my condition. And so I thought. What if I offer her a really nice life? What if I build her a seriously lovely home? What if I keep her in the best car on the Blakely showroom floor and buy her all the pretty things that women seem to like so much? What if I did all that?"

Jason reached up and wiped away the lone tear snaking down his scarred cheek. "Would that make up for all that I can't offer her anymore? But you don't need any of that." He sat back down on the sofa. "You come from money and you have money of your own. Everything I could offer you is something you already have."

"You're right. I don't need any of that." She sat next to him and took his hand between hers. "Although it means a lot to me that you want so badly to give it to me." She lifted the hand she was holding and kissed it. "But Jason, there is something you can offer me, something that I need and want more than anything in the world. That something is you. Just offer me yourself."

"But that's not enough. I have to be able to offer you something more. Something to make up for the deficits." He pulled his hand away.

Exasperated, she tried again. "Everybody has deficits. It's just that yours are more visible." She shook her head. "It's ironic, you know. I didn't tell you about the damned trust fund because I wanted you to love me for myself, not my money. You know, I want to do the same thing for you. Love you for yourself, not the money you bring home or the material possessions you lay at my feet. Damn it, Jason, I love you for who you are and not what you can give me. And that's what I want from you. Your love. And nothing else."

"It's just not enough. My love and nothing else. It's just not enough for a woman like you. You deserve better than that."

"Damn it, Jason, that's just your insecurity talking," Thoroughly put out and not trying to hide it, she insisted, "Your love is more than enough for me. But I'm not going to argue with you about it. Instead I am going to issue a challenge to you. I challenge you and I dare you, Jason Donahue, to think about the way you feel about me. I want you to think about the way you love me. Then I want you to ask yourself if there is another man anywhere on this planet that will love me the way you do, that will give me the kind of love you give me or will be the kind of partner to me you would. When you come up with the answer, I hope you will have the courage to come to me and offer yourself and your love to me. Because that's what I want from you. Your love. That's all I've ever wanted from you and that's all I will ever want."

Jason stared at her for a long minute then leaned over and kissed her sweetly and gently. Then he rose to his feet and walked to the door. "I wish I could believe you. That my love would really be enough."

"You can believe it." She turned to face him. "Think about it. Promise me you'll think about it."

Jason nodded. "I promise. I will definitely think about it."

* * *

Jason turned on the coffee maker and started setting up chairs. For the second week in a row his mind wasn't really on the support group. It hadn't been on his job, either, and he'd let a couple of sales slip through his fingers that should have been slam dunks.

He'd spent the week thinking about the challenge Emily issued and what he should do about it. He so wanted to take her up on her offer. He did love her. He loved her beyond reason. But there was bound to be another man out there who would love her just as much, a man with youth and health and looks that could bring so much more to the table than Jason ever could.

So he hadn't called her back. He'd even gone so far as to find another apartment all the way across town so that their paths would no longer cross on a regular basis. It was killing him to be away from her, but if he couldn't have her, couldn't give her what she deserved in a man, it was better for the both of them not to see one another anymore.

Jason knew he wasn't the only one who would be hurting tonight. He had neither seen nor heard from Zach since the last meeting, and Jason wondered if Zach would even show up tonight. Although he was dreading hearing the story and coping with the aftermath, Jason hoped Zach would come to let his friends get him through what was bound to be a painful episode in his life.

So what do I do? Did he tell them he had a fiasco of his own to share? Did he merely say that things didn't work out and they moved on? He'd cross that bridge when he came to it.

As always, he stood at the door and greeted each member. Nope, no Zach tonight, he thought as the last of the stragglers poured themselves coffee and ate a couple of the homemade cookies Hillary brought. They were seated and Joel was telling the group about his online research into PA schools when Zach and Rosalee burst through the door carrying a decorated cake and several bottles of champagne.

"Sorry we're late, but the bakery wasn't done with putting the finishing touches on the cake," Rosalee gushed. "I hope we have time at the end for a little celebration." She put down the cake and held up her finger where Zach's engagement ring sparkled brightly.

"S-she said 'yes,'" Zach exclaimed.

"And we wanted you to share in our joy." Rosalee's face was wreathed in a smile as wide as Texas.

"To hell with the support meeting," Joel crowed. "Let's have us a party tonight!"

She said yes? Rosalee was going to marry Zach?

Jason snapped his jaw shut to keep his mouth from falling open in shock. Quickly, he added his congratulations to the others being offered as he tried and failed to wrap his head around it.

Sure, he was delighted, truly delighted that this beautiful young woman was going to marry Zach. But at the same time he couldn't understand it, not in the least. Wouldn't she want a man who could offer her more than Zach could?

The cake was cut and the champagne poured, and the meeting did indeed turn into a party, a loud, happy party honoring Zach and Rosalee. It was late when it finally broke up, but as usual Zach and Rosalee insisted on staying and helping Jason put things away.

Rosalee cut Jason a big piece of the leftover cake. She sent Zach to their car with the rest and the leftover wine and plastic champagne glasses. Jason watched pensively as Zach, still smiling like a fool, disappeared out the door.

"You know, I'm really happy for him," he said to Rosalee. "I was terrified when he brought that ring in last week. I wasn't sure you would want to marry him in the shape that he's in."

"You and most of the rest of the world," Rosalee agreed. "My mother's appalled. She's firmly convinced we'll end up back in the trailer park she worked so hard for me to get out of."

Jason laughed. "I doubt you'll have to go back there." His face sobered. "I guess she just doesn't understand."

"And from the look on your face, neither do you. Look, Jason, I'll be the first one to admit Zach can't bring to a union what somebody like you can. He'll never get his degree or get a job like yours, and he will never have what a man like you has to offer a woman. But he brings to me the best of himself, Jason, and that's his love for me. He's giving me everything he has." Rosalee stopped and wiped a tear from her cheek. "And that's quite enough for me."

He'll never have what I have to offer. He's giving her the best of himself. He's giving her everything he has. That was what was important to the surprisingly wise Rosalee—Zach's love.

"I think I get it now," Jason said slowly. He leaned down and kissed Rosalee's cheek. "I think I get a lot of things now."

Finally, he understood, watching Zach and Rosalee drive away from the church parking lot. He understood why Rosalee was marrying Zach. As little as Zach could bring to the marriage, he would bring Rosalee his love.

So what about you, you wussy coward? If Zach has the courage to offer Rosalee his love and Rosalee has the courage to accept it, why can't you and Emily do the same?

Rosalee's words echoed in Jason's head as he started his engine and headed toward his new apartment. Rosalee thought he would be a good catch, with a degree and a good job. And maybe he would be at that. So what if he was older than Emily and looked like hell? So what if he'd never be as rich as the Harringtons or the Rileys? He could still take care of her and build her a nice house. But mostly he could love her, love her like no other man ever would or could. That was the best of Jason Donahue, the love he felt for his Em. That was his everything. And he could by God offer that to her. According to her, that was all she really wanted anyway.

Jason picked up his phone and started to call her, but as he drove down University Drive and glanced over at the tree-filled campus, he put the phone back down on the seat. He would not go over to her apartment tonight. She deserved better in a marriage proposal than a visit on a Tuesday evening. She deserved to know just how much he loved her and how special she was to him.

He knew just how to do it. And he had a lot of phone calls to make.

Chapter Ten

Emily leaned her head back on the sofa and closed the three-ring binder containing her advanced molecular genetics notes for the semester. This exam was one of the two finals she still had to take before she could pack a suitcase and head home to San Antonio for the holidays and nearly a month of Patsy's good cooking.

Most years she was chomping at the bit to take that last exam and get in the car, but this year she was in no hurry to go home for Christmas. In fact, she was in no hurry to do much of anything remotely related to the bustling delight of the holiday season. It was as though a pall had settled over her existence, robbing her of her usual enthusiasm and cheer and replacing it with a wintry gray blanket of gloom that had nothing to do with the sparkling sunshine outside her windows. That blanket of doom got deeper and darker every day that went by without word from Jason.

He wasn't coming back, she thought as she fished a sugar-free soda out of the refrigerator. It had been two weeks since he came to talk and she issued him the challenge. At first she had been hopeful; surely he would see that no man would ever love her the way that he did and that he belonged by her side. But as the days went by and Jason didn't call, the horrible truth began to sink in. He was going to let her go. He was going to let go of everything they had together because of his own insecurity. He was convinced that he was a bad bargain and that she could do better. Not wanting to give up on them, she had even knocked on his door and demanded to see him, but when Benny said he'd moved out and they didn't know where he was, any hope she'd harbored of reconciliation was shattered.

Jason was gone, really gone from her life, and she had better get used to the fact.

She sat down on the front porch steps to drink her soda. She was draining the last of it when a cherry-red Mustang convertible with the top down turned the corner and a familiar face waved from the front seat.

"Holly!"

She jumped up as her sister swung the car into the driveway then met her in a huge embrace. "What are you doing here, and where did you get this fantastic car?"

Holly hugged Emily tightly. "I'm here to spend the weekend and show off my Christmas present from Jimmy. Isn't it something else?"

Emily stepped back and eyed the brand-spanking-new car. "Sweet, real sweet. So this was your Christmas present, huh? Some present."

"Yeah, it was for Christmas. And the fact that last week the Miata laid down in the highway and wouldn't get up again may have had something to do with it. Carrie and I had to wait almost an hour before anybody could get there to rescue us."

"Ouch. Yep, I'd say it was time for a new car. So what prompted a long trip down the highway when I'm sure you have Christmas shopping to do?"

"Trying out the car, mostly. But Patsy said you were kind of down and I thought you might could use a little sisterly company. Jimmy and Carrie are Christmas shopping with Janelle in San Antonio and won't miss me."

Emily blinked back tears. "It's so good of you to come. Thanks."

"So let me make a pit stop in your facilities and I'll take you for a short spin."

Holly's short spin turned in to the better part of three hours as they ended up driving all the way to Crockett and back in the cool, bright December sunshine.

Emily could feel the cobwebs blowing away and the gray fog lifting as the wind whistled in her ears and the sun beat down on her face. She and Holly made no real attempt to talk as they flew past the towering oak and pine trees of East Texas. Emily let herself soak up the soothing atmosphere of the majestic old forest.

She needed this, she thought as the miles flew by. She needed a break. She needed to get away from her problems for a while and soak up some sweet, sweet peace.

It was nearing sunset as she and Holly pulled back into College Station. Holly took the wide boulevard that would take them past the campus. "Say, how about some barbeque at Tom's?" Holly asked cheerfully.

"Where? They went out of business years ago," Emily said. "Right after you graduated, I think."

"Damn. Has it been that long since I've been back here?" Holly made a rueful face. "So where would you like to eat?"

They ended up at one of Emily's favorite Mexican hole-in-the-wall cafes. Their server brought tostadas and salsa and they ordered typical Tex-Mex plates of tacos and enchiladas. After the server left with their order, Holly turned to Emily, her face suddenly serious. "You want to talk about things or just let it slide?"

"It would be easier to let it slide, but we can talk about it if you'd like to know what happened."

"Yes, I would like to know, for more than one reason. I like Jason and will probably continue to work with him and his support group. Also I'm wanting to know cuz I'd hate for the same thing to happen to another nice couple that really belongs together if I could say or do something to prevent it."

"There's not too much chance of it happening all that often," Emily said dryly. "Four-and-a-half-million-dollar trust funds are not exactly thick on the ground."

Holly looked at Emily shrewdly. "Are you sure the money's the problem?"

"Not all of the problem, certainly, but it sure didn't make things any better. Jason already had the inferiority complex from hell because of his appearance, and finding out about the money was just too much. He's got this idea that he's no bargain in the marriage market because of his injuries and the scarring and that he has to do something to make up for that if he's going to be any kind of husband."

"And the 'making it up' piece was going to be clothes and cars and a house to die for," Holly stated. "He said as much to me on Thanksgiving, before Granddad pulled his little stunt. He wanted to ask you to marry him but was already so damn scared you'd say no that he was stalling. And that was before he found out about the money. That damned trust fund didn't have as much to do with things as Jason's insecurity did."

"I think I know that," Emily said. "But why is he so damned insecure? You aren't."

Holly looked at Emily and didn't even try to hide her astonishment. "What in the world ever gave you an idea like that? Don't you remember the shape I was in last year when I first got out of the hospital?"

"Well, sure. But that was then. You're not insecure anymore," Emily protested.

"Damned if that's so," Holly asserted. "I'll admit it's not as bad as it was at first or when I started seeing Jimmy, but once in a while I watch some graceful woman glide across the floor or catch a glimpse of my limp in a big mirror or struggle to do something with my left hand and I'll wonder what Jimmy's doing with me, why he hasn't gone out and found some physically perfect woman to love. You know what? Sometimes he feels the same way. He fretted for a solid week after that flashback he had over Thanksgiving, afraid I would get tired of his PTSD issues and kick him to the curb."

"I never thought about that," Emily murmured.

"Oh, yeah. We all are plagued with it. Every damned one of us who came home from war different than we were before. You want to learn a little bit more about insecurity and the wounded warrior? Sit in on a few of my group's support meetings. Or go with Jason to some of his. Ninety percent of what we talk about at those meetings is insecurity. We look different, or we move different, or we can't do everything that we could do before. That does a number on our self-confidence. It's that much harder when we jump or get pushed back in the dating pool and find ourselves competing with men and women who aren't injured and have the self-confidence we got robbed of. And the hell of it is that even those of us who are with other wounded warriors are insecure. It's another part of the aftermath."

"And how long does this insecurity last?" Emily asked quietly.

"Every damned day for the rest of our lives, as far as I can tell. We don't get over it; we just learn to push past it and go on with our lives."

"And I guess Jason hasn't pushed past his yet," Emily said thoughtfully.

"Not completely, no," Holly agreed "He's better, obviously, but that sweet man has a long, long way to go before he's able to push past it completely."

"So what do I do?" Emily asked. "The last time I talked I sort of left the ball in his court."

"For crying out loud, you don't leave the ball in his court! If you wait for him to come around you'll wait forever. You need to talk to him again," Holly said firmly. "You need to remind him of how much you love him and how much you need him, and you keep hammering it home to him until he gets it through his thick head that you really do mean it. Then, when the insecurity raises its ugly head again, as it will, you remind him some more and help him force that insecurity right back down where it belongs."

"I'd be more than willing to do that if I even knew where he was," Emily said ruefully. "He moved out and didn't tell Wade and Benny where he was going."

Holly shrugged. "You can track him down and talk to him after Christmas. Or who knows? You might get up the nerve to go to Blakely's."

"Not likely," Emily said doubtfully.

"Well, we'll see. And in the meantime, I want you to take me to church tomorrow morning. To that big one, you know. The one right off campus. The one I went to sometimes when I was a student here."

"Church? Since when do you want to go to church? You haven't done church in years."

"Trip down memory lane, maybe? Need to get back in the habit for Jimmy and Carrie? Besides, I have a hell of a lot to be thankful for these days and maybe I'd like to say a little prayer letting the good Lord know how I feel."

"Sure, we can go to church," Emily said. And while she was there, she could send up a few prayers of her own, prayers that somehow she could find her way back to Jason, and that he would find his way back to her and her love.

* * *

Emily sat beside Holly on the hard wooden pew and stared up at the sun beaming through the stained glass windows behind the chancel.

The brightly colored windows sparkled in the morning sunlight, and almost against her will Emily felt herself casting off her disappointment and despair and replacing it with a fragile, tentative hope.

Holly was right. Emily needed to talk to Jason again. She needed to do more to convince him that he was wrong about himself, that he was a good bargain in the marriage market, and, mostly, that they belonged together. It wouldn't be that hard to track him down; if she had to, she would park in his office at the dealership and stay parked until he agreed to give their relationship the chance it deserved. *He still might say no*, she thought as the pastor's mellow delivery flowed melodically around her ears. He still might insist that she deserved better than him. But she wasn't going to make it easy for him to turn her away.

The minister bowed his head and Emily whispered a little prayer, asking that Jason not give up on them. Communion was offered and the offering was collected and the benediction sung, and Holly and Emily made their way to the back of the sanctuary and shook hands with the minister. They got in the Mustang and Holly gestured toward the Texas A&M campus right across the street. "Do we have time for a walk around campus? I haven't been back since I graduated."

"That surprises me, with both of your other brothers on the football team," Emily said as she and Holly walked toward the corner where they could cross the wide, busy thoroughfare on a light. "Russ has come back to a bunch of the football games. He thinks Graham and Sullivan are both dynamite players."

"It was easy for him to get here when he was stationed at Fort Hood. Remember, I was never stationed anywhere near campus. Maybe Jimmy and I can bring Carrie to a few games next season. I do need to see the twins play before they graduate."

Holly parked close to the quad where she spent her A&M years in the Corps of Cadets, and the sisters began a leisurely stroll through the beautiful, sprawling old campus, with its interesting hodge-podge of old and new buildings, grassy expanses and shady sidewalks lined with huge live oak trees. The skirt of Emily's new turquoise dress, the one Holly brought for her Christmas gift and practically insisted she wear this morning, swirled around her legs in the breeze as they strolled down the sidewalk.

Holly immediately began asking about the changes that had occurred in the campus since her days as a student and Emily obligingly answered them. Holly spent a few minutes on the quad itself, lost in memories, and when Emily asked her what she was thinking about she admitted she was remembering several of her old friends from the Corps of Cadets who hadn't made it home from Iraq or Afghanistan.

"I try to stress to my wounded warriors that, injuries and all, we were lucky to make it home alive," Holly mused. "Not everybody did."

"I think Jason preaches the same sermon in his support group. I just wish he always believed it."

Holly glanced over at Emily. "Oh, I think he does." Then Holly steered Emily away from the quad and toward the heart of the campus. "Come on, I want to see a little more from my glory days before my leg gives out on me."

Obliging, Emily followed along with the again-chattering Holly as they strolled toward the center of the campus. They were almost to the academic building, the huge domed, pillared white stone building at the heart of the campus, when Emily caught sight of a couple of cadets in full uniform carrying their sabers, hot-footing it down the sidewalk, and a cluster of people gathered under the oak trees lining the sidewalk that led to the famous Century Tree. The huge oak tree was over a hundred years old and the site of countless proposals as generations of Aggies, complete with an honor guard and an arch of raised sabers, asked their sweethearts to be their wives.

"Uh-oh, you know what this means," Emily laughed.

"Yeah, some poor bastard's waiting down at the end of the sidewalk under the Century Tree sweating bullets." Holly grinned. "A Century Tree proposal. How utterly romantic."

"You still think so, after all the times you had to stand out in the hot sun and hold up a sword?"

"Of course. I used to love them. Still do."

Emily peered down the sidewalk. "I wonder who the lucky girl is today," she said wistfully.

"Well, why don't we get a little closer and see who she is? You know they won't mind."

Not giving Emily a chance to object, Holly started down the sidewalk. They could see the honor guard of Cadets assembling themselves a few yards down from the tree and the bench nestled at its base. As they got a little closer the family and friends gathered under the trees started to come into focus and Emily could feel her heart start to pound in her throat.

Wade and Benny were standing there, grinning from ear to ear. Jimmy Adamcik was holding Carrie's hand and juggling a camera. Her best friend from high school stood beside her old roommates from her freshman year. They were holding their boyfriends' hands and giving her a thumbs-up sign.

Jason's entire support group stood together a little to one side with smiles on their faces. A tall man with Jason's bone structure stood next to a pretty woman wiping happy tears from eyes as blue as Jason's.

Kevin and Tess had their children on their shoulders so the little ones could see. Her smiling parents stood next to her grandparents, and Russ, resplendent in his dress blues, stood beside the honor guard.

And, waiting on the other side of the honor guard, dressed in his most formal suit and clutching a single red rose in his hand, stood a solemn-faced Jason.

"Oh my God," Emily breathed as she started to tremble. This was for her! *She* was the girl receiving the marriage proposal this afternoon.

Holly's face broke into a megawatt smile as she pulled Emily close and gave her a swift hug. "I do believe the lucky girl today is you, Emily. Jason's old Cadet Company wanted to do this for him." She let go then nodded her head to Russ. "It's time. Go on, Emily. Jason's waiting for you. Don't make him wait any longer."

Russ stepped forward and offered his arm. Emily trembled as she hooked her hand around his elbow.

She couldn't believe it. Jason was here. Jason had found it within himself to overcome his fear and his insecurity. He had found the courage to offer himself and his love to her—and in the most public way possible, asking her to be his wife.

Her happiness was almost too much to bear; she could feel tears of joy spring to her eyes. Her mother quickly shoved a tissue into her hand and the cadets snapped their swords into the traditional arch.

"Shall we?" Russ asked, his eyes sparkling and his grin wide. "Let's go put that terrified SOB out of his misery."

Emily nodded, her eyes on Jason as Russ escorted her beneath the raised swords. They reached the end of the honor guard and Jason held out his hand. Russ released his sister and turned to Jason, his eyes dancing with devilment.

"Take good care of her, you hear? You can start with that fancy-assed house you're gonna build her."

Jason and Emily looked at one another and laughed. Only Russ would come out with something like that at a time like this. His face sobering, Jason handed Emily the rose and tipped her face up toward his.

"I'll build you the house, but first things first," he said as he covered her lips in the sweetest kiss Emily had ever had. "I love you, Emily. I love you so much."

"I love you too, Jason," she said as her tears of joy spilled from her eyes and ran down her cheeks.

Jason's eyes were suspiciously moist. "I was afraid you wouldn't anymore, after I lost faith in us. I'm glad you didn't give up on me." Jason escorted her down the sidewalk to the bench beneath the towering old tree. He took the tissue and blotted the tears off Emily's cheeks. "I wasn't trying to make you cry."

"I always cry when I'm happy."

"Still." Jason pointed and Emily sat down on the bench. Jason sat down beside her and took her by the hand. "Emily, I just want it on record that I still don't think I'm enough for you. I will never be enough for you and even if I work my ass off every day for the rest of my life, I will never be able to give you all I think you deserve."

He slipped down off the bench and knelt on one knee in front of her. "But I will give you everything I am and everything I have and every bit of the love I have within me. That's the best of me, and I'm offering it to you. And if you think that's enough, I would be a damn fool not to take you up on that.

"Emily Louise Riley, will you do me the honor of becoming my wife?"

She nodded. "Of course I will. I love you, Jason, and will treasure you always."

Jason got up off his knee and sat back down on the bench. He took an older-looking ring box from his front coat pocket and carefully opened the lid. Inside, a pair of blood-red rubies were surrounded by a delicate filigree of lacy platinum. "It was my grandmother's," he said softly. He gestured to her hand. "May I?"

She held up her hand and he slipped the ring on her finger. They stood up together, both smiling as their friends and family clapped and shouted their approval. He offered his arm and together they walked toward the arch of swords raised high in the sky for them.

Jason looked down at Emily and smiled at her. "I still wish I could give you more."

Emily tipped her chin up and cradled his face, so scarred and so precious.

"Jason, don't you understand? You've just given me the world."

ABOUT THE AUTHOR

The author of twenty romance novels, Emily Mims combined her writing career with a career in public education until leaving the classroom to write full time. The mother of two sons, now she and her husband Charles split their time between central Texas and eastern Tennessee. For relaxation she plays the piano, organ, dulcimer, and ukulele. She says, "I love to write romances because I believe in them. Romance happened to me and it can happen to any woman—if she'll just let it."

Did you enjoy this book? Drop us a line and say so! We love to hear from readers, and so do our authors. To connect, visit www.boroughspublishinggroup.com online, send comments directly to info@boroughspublishinggroup.com, or friend us on Facebook and Twitter. And be sure to check back regularly for contests and new releases in your favorite subgenres of romance!

Are you an aspiring writer? Check out www.boroughspublishinggroup.com/submit and see if we can help you make your dreams come true.

www.ingramcontent.com/pod-product-compliance
Lightning Source LLC
Chambersburg PA
CBHW060642130626
46555CB00002B/922